Henry Cecil was the pseudon
Leon. He was born in Norwɩ ⸱ ⸱⸱⸱⸱⸱ Ʞecɩory, near
London, England in 1902. He studied at Cambridge
where he edited an undergraduate magazine and wrote a
Footlights May Week production. Called to the bar in
1923, he served with the British Army during the Second
World War. While in the Middle East with his battalion he
used to entertain the troops with a serial story each
evening. This formed the basis of his first book, *Full Circle*.
He was appointed a County Court Judge in 1949 and held
that position until 1967. The law and the circumstances
which surround it were the source of his many novels,
plays, and short stories. His books are works of great
comic genius with unpredictable twists of plot which
highlight the often absurd workings of the English legal
system. He died in 1976.

To Lynda
with love +

UNLAWFUL
OCCASIONS

by

Henry Cecil

gratitude for
all kindness + help
Affectionately

Barbara
(widow of Henry
Cecil

HOUSE OF STRATUS

This edition published in 2000 by House of Stratus, an imprint of Stratus Holdings plc, 24c Old Burlington Street, London, W1X 1RL, UK.

www.houseofstratus.com

Typeset, printed and bound by House of Stratus.

A catalogue record for this book is available from the British Library.

ISBN 1-84232-067-X

Contents

CHAPTER ONE

Prologue

'Prisoner at the bar,' said the clerk, 'you have been convicted of felony. Have you anything to say why sentence should not be passed upon you according to law?'

The prisoner cleared his throat, but need not have bothered. He was not meant to answer the question, though it was not unreasonable for him to think that he was. Surely, he might well have thought, the question was intended, if not to give him the chance of repeating that he was not guilty, at least of delivering an impassioned plea for mercy? But the fact that he may have had no real chance in life since his birth, that his father may have been hanged and his mother may have been a drug addict, that he may have served with distinction in the war (except during a short period of desertion) and that he was severely tempted to commit the crime of which he has been convicted, is totally irrelevant. It would even be irrelevant for him to claim that it was Brown who committed the crime and that he himself was a hundred miles away at the time, and that would be just as irrelevant even if it were true and the conviction amounted to a miscarriage of justice. There are, in fact, other ways of dealing with a miscarriage of justice but the sole object of the question is to give the prisoner the opportunity of what is called 'moving in arrest of judgment,' a technical procedure which is only justified in a tiny minority of cases – not one in ten thousand.

In practice, however, prisoners are allowed to make pleas for mercy or even to reiterate their protestations of innocence. The alternative would be to try to explain to a prisoner what is meant by moving in arrest of judgment, and this might be difficult and would take time. For example, the prisoner, having been asked the question whether he has anything to say etc., would be interrupted by the clerk or the judge as soon as he began his answer, with something like: 'You can't say that.'

'Why not? You asked me, and I'm telling you.'

It is normally quicker to let the prisoner have his say and to ignore what he says.

So the prisoner who had cleared his throat was allowed to speak. But he did not make the usual kind of plea.

'My Lord,' he said, 'I cannot give any reason why sentence should *not* be passed, but I should like to mention several reasons why it *should*. Blackmail is, as you, my Lord, so rightly mentioned to the jury – more than once, if I may say so – in your summing up, blackmail is moral murder. I showed no mercy to my victims, so I need expect none from you. I have been practising my iniquitous trade for a number of years and have managed to salt away a tidy sum, none of which has been discovered or will be returned. I propose to live on it after I come out. Whether I then return to my previous calling or not will depend upon several factors – how much I like it in prison, what else I can find to do when I come out, and so forth. But I'm afraid it is early days to consider that matter. Am I sorry for what I have done? Not in the least. I have done very well out of it and the people

I robbed were all criminals. Otherwise I should not have been able to rob them. I am, of course, sorry that I have been caught, but at least I have learned one or two lessons in the process, which I shall bear in mind if I decide to continue along the same lines when I come out. I can find no redeeming feature in my case, except perhaps this. That I have said everything your Lordship was going to say, and so saved you the trouble. Perhaps I should add – again to save your Lordship trouble – that you can't give me more than the maximum which was no doubt provided for people like me.'

Mr Justice Denby was not a brilliant judge, but he could take a hint.

'You will go to prison for fourteen years,' he said.

'As I thought,' said the prisoner before they led him away. 'My guess was as good as yours.'

Later that evening Brian Culsworth QC, who had led the prosecution against the man, discussed the case with the judge over the port.

'I've never taken a liking to a blackmailer before,' said Culsworth, 'but I must say my heart warmed to this one when he made that little speech.'

'It was quite as good as I could have done,' said the judge. 'He didn't leave a thing out. But what a scoundrel. Clever, though.'

'I'm surprised,' said Culsworth, 'that a man as able as that should take to blackmail. If he has to indulge in crime, I should have thought that fraud or something of the kind would have been preferable from his point of view. In the first place he'd have more chance of getting off and secondly, if he is caught, the sentence wouldn't be anything like as great.'

'But he took it all very calmly,' said the judge. 'I confess that, if I knew I was about to get fourteen years, I shouldn't be so perky about it. He might have been seeing someone off on a train for all the anxiety he displayed. At the best he won't be out for over nine years. It's a long time, even if you have a nest-egg waiting for you when you come out.'

'It's the easy money, I suppose, which tempted him,' said Culsworth. 'D'you remember that burglar who was tried years ago with a lot of others for blackmail? He said in mitigation that he was a burglar by trade, that it was a difficult and not very remunerative job and full of danger, and that when he saw these others making so much more so easily he fell for it.'

'Yes, I remember the case. The ringleader got imprisonment for life. He was an able chap too. Spoke several languages and could easily have earned an honest living. It's not exciting enough for some people, I imagine, while others can't stand regular hours of work.'

'Well, if I went in for crime I'd certainly never try blackmail,' said Culsworth. 'Every man against you, including the judge when it comes to passing sentence.'

'Come to think of it,' said the judge, 'I might have given him fourteen years on each count and made them run consecutively – forty-two years in all. Why didn't I think of that?'

Brian Culsworth was one of the leading silks who practised to a large extent in crime. The danger of having a criminal practice is not that association with criminals tends to lead barristers into crime themselves, but that so much licence is allowed to those who represent people accused of crime that it is sometimes abused. And, indeed, there has possibly been a tendency for some barristers at the criminal Bar to think that in defending a prisoner no holds are barred. Culsworth himself had the highest reputation and his integrity had never been even remotely questioned. He had developed a large practice and at the time of the prosecution of the blackmailer he was probably at the happiest stage of his career. Except for the amount of work which he had to do, and which necessarily deprived him of seeing as much of his family as he would have liked, everything was well. And even this one disadvantage would probably not last very much longer. There was every chance of his being appointed a High Court judge. He had, of course, had periods of disappointment and unhappiness in his life, but now everything seemed set fair.

No one would have thought at that moment that a dispute between a man called Leslie Baker and a workmate, over a football pool win, was soon to cause Culsworth the greatest concern and to make him believe that his whole career was ruined.

CHAPTER TWO

Mr Baker

Leslie Baker looked moodily into the fire and remained silent for about ten minutes. As he was normally a cheerful and talkative person at home, his wife had spoken to him several times during the silence but without result.

'What is the matter, Les?' she said again, 'You're giving me the creeps.'

'Creeps,' repeated Mr Baker, 'that's about the word – creep. Creep, creep, creep,' he almost shouted.

His wife became anxious, almost frightened.

'D'you think you ought to see the doctor, dear?' she said tentatively.

She had never been frightened of her husband before. He was the best of husbands, and his only idiosyncrasy was a curious and obstinate resentment of authority. But he was consistent and did not abuse his own authority at home. Could he have gone out of his mind?

'Creep,' repeated her husband. 'Creep, creep, creep. Where's Andy?' he said suddenly.

'In his bedroom doing his homework, dear.'

'Andy,' shouted Mr Baker, but before Mrs Baker could make up her mind whether her husband's mind had really turned and he was going to slit their throats, Andy came in.

'Hullo, pa,' he said. 'What's up?'

He, like the rest of the family, had never had reason to be frightened of his father, but although loud angry words were unheard of in the Baker family, shouting was the normal method of communication from room to room. Some children are brought up to talk, others to shout. The Bakers shouted. It was the friendliest possible shouting and, as nearly all their neighbours did the same, the noise was no cause of discord. The few who did not shout accepted the inevitable, like Londoners on an air route, and quickly got used to it. Or went away.

'Well, pa?' said Andy encouragingly, while Mrs Baker rather anxiously looked around the room for a weapon of defence in case the worst happened.

'When you swear at school,' said Mr Baker, 'what do they let you say?'

'Come again, pa,' said Andy.

'It's a good school we've sent you to,' said Mr Baker, 'and I'm sure they wouldn't let you say anything that wasn't fit for your ma to hear. What do they teach you now?'

'Teach us, pa?' said Andy a little puzzled, 'teach us? Oh – lots of things. Physics, chemistry, history ...'

'No, no,' interrupted Mr Baker, 'swear words, I mean. What do they teach you?'

'Teach us swear words!' said Andy. 'Come off it, pa.'

It was Mr Baker's turn to appear surprised.

'Well, don't they, son?' he asked.

'Course not.'

'Well, I'll be ...' but Mr Baker just managed to stop himself. His lips had formed themselves into the necessary position for a 'b,' but he was able to control his breath. But even Mrs Baker, who had never in her life heard her husband swear, could not fail to see what had nearly happened. Well, it was better than slitting their throats, but something serious must be the matter.

'Look, son,' said Mr Baker, 'don't they teach you nothing but learning? Don't they teach you how to speak and how to behave?'

'They think you and mum do that, pa.'

'How can we do it? We ain't never been educated. If a man wants to swear in front of his wife, what can he say now? Surely they teach you that? We all know what not to say, but there must be something that people like you're going to be when you grow up can say? What do the masters say when they get wild?'

'Well, I did once hear one of them say "Take that bloody grin off your face." '

'Now look here, Andy,' said Mr Baker sternly, 'I'm not having that language in this house.'

'Sorry, pa, but you asked me.'

'I didn't expect you to say that, not in front of your ma. Say you're sorry now.'

'Sorry, ma. He left the next term, though.'

'I should think so,' said Mr Baker.

'But what d'you want to know all about it for, pa?' asked Andy.

'Don't worry your pa,' said Mrs Baker, 'he's upset about something.'

'Upset!' said Mr Baker. 'I'm upset all right. The – the – now what can I say? There are times when a man wouldn't be human if he didn't want to swear.'

'Go on, pa, have a go,' encouraged Andy.

'Andy, behave yourself,' said Mrs Baker. 'You'd better go back to your room.'

'No, don't go, Andy. You've got to hear it too. The creep. Creep, creep, creep.'

Mrs Baker was now regaining confidence. That something was seriously wrong she realised, but her husband had exhibited no signs of violence.

'What is it, dear?' she asked.

'Chelsea drew away,' said Mr Baker. 'Doncaster drew at home.'

'Oh dear,' said Mrs Baker, who now thought she realised what the trouble was. Every week her husband went in for the pools. Not to any great extent, but regularly. Every week he lost. Not to any great extent, but regularly. Every now and then he would behave as almost every gambler does – if only I'd put Doncaster to win away, or Chelsea at home – whatever made me do the opposite of what I knew was going to happen, and so on and so forth. If only – if only. Well probably this was the closest he'd ever had to a win – if only he'd done something which he hadn't done, or not done something he had done. Mrs Baker stopped her thoughts. Her husband, though not a very religious man, would not have any of his family make fun of the Church or its services – which they attended more than most people – and she was sure he wouldn't approve of thinking of football pools and the General Confession at the same time.

'How many points did you get?' she asked sympathetically.

'I got the lot,' said Mr Baker without enthusiasm. And then, with sudden fury: 'I got the blinking lot. Twenty-four points. Twenty-four perishing points.'

Horror, thought Mrs Baker, he forgot to post it. Or did I? If she was the guilty party, she deserved to have her throat slit. Twenty-four points. First prize. It could never happen again.

'What's the divi going to be?' asked Andy. 'I suppose too many other blokes have got it too.'

'Well, they won't have,' said Mr Baker. 'Didn't I tell you Chelsea and Doncaster both drew? That was against the form. It'll be sixty thousand I shouldn't wonder. Big money, anyway. The creep. I'd like to …'

'Then you did post it?' said Mrs Baker.

'I did not,' said Mr Baker, 'but he did – the perishing oh, for pity's sake, give me some of those words they don't teach you at school.'

'Who posted it, dear, and why won't you get the money?'

'Look,' said Mr Baker, 'I'll tell you. There's a chap at the works called Potter. We used to have one at the boozer on the way home sometimes. And last week we got talking about the pools. He showed me his coupon. And I suddenly had an idea. "Look, Potty," I said, "what's the good of following the papers? Lots of people follow them. So, if they're right, the divi's nothing."

'I looked at his coupon.

' "Tell you what I mean," I said, and then I stopped. "Look, old son," I said, "let's share this one together. I've sent mine in."

' "OK" he says. "Now, what's your plan?"

' "Well, look," I say. "All these 'ere papers put Chelsea as a dead cert to lose away and Doncaster as a dead cert to win at home. Put 'em both as draws."

'Well, he does that and we fill in the rest of the six much as everyone else. And blow me down, it turns up. The whole blooming lot, twenty-four points. There are only nine draws anyway. So we're in the money. As soon as I heard, I went straight from work to his home. "Hullo," he says, not too affable. "Haven't you seen?" I says. "Seen what?" he says. "The results." "Results of what?" he says, all cool like. My tummy feels like when they declared war last time, or was it the war before? Anyway, I could feel what was coming, but of course I didn't let on. "The pools, Potty," I says, "the pools." "Now it's odd you should mention the pools," he says, "because I've just had a bit of luck." "*You've* just had a bit of luck. *We've* just had a bit of luck you mean." "Why, have you won too?" he says. "What a coincidence. Congratulations. Sure you posted the letter? I once knew a chap who didn't. It was dreadful." "See here, Potty," I says, "it's you who posted the letter." "If it's me you're worrying about," he says, "you needn't. I posted it all right." "Well then," I says, "we've won." "How come?" he says, all cool still. I could 'ave smashed his perishing face. "You win on your coupon, I win on mine. But I didn't post yours, old cock. You did that yourself, – or didn't." Well, you can see what's happened. The … the … perisher says we didn't agree to go in together and is going to stick to the lot.'

'The – ,' and Andy nearly said a word which was definitely not allowed at his school.

'But surely,' said Mrs Baker, 'you can make him share?'

'How?' asked Mr Baker. 'That's what I'd like to know. How? You wouldn't have me bash it out of him, would you? I'd end up in jail, or hospital, or both.'

'But it's criminal.'

'You're telling me.'

'Well, you can have the law on him, can't you?'

'That's just what I can't do, see. There's only his word against mine and anyway the law don't have nothing to do with betting and such like. It's what they call a matter of honour. Honour, I ask you. I'd like to push his honour down his throat, with his false teeth.'

'Well, it's a bleeding shame,' said Andy, 'and I don't see why you should stand for it.'

For once his father's reproof only took the form of a slight amendment.

'It is a perishing shame,' he corrected.

Ten minutes later Andy made an excuse for going out and went to the police station. Half an hour later he arrived back home in a state of great excitement.

'It's all right,' he said, as soon as his parents asked him what he'd been doing. 'You can make him pay. I went down and saw the sergeant, and he telephoned a solicitor. This chap had had just the same type of case and won it. He says it's quite definite. If two blokes go into a pool together and one of them pockets the money the other one can definitely go to Court about it.'

'Well, there you are,' said Mrs Baker happily. 'Didn't I say something could be done?'

'I don't much like the law,' said Mr Baker, 'and anyway it's still only my word against his.'

'But they must believe you, Les,' said Mrs Baker. 'You never tell a lie.'

'I don't like judges and suchlike,' said Mr Baker.

'You like Mr Potter less,' said Andy.

'All right, I'll go and see this solicitor chap anyway. What's his name?'

'I didn't catch. But the sergeant'll tell you.'

'Well, good for you, Andy,' said Mr Baker. 'I can't say I'm all that hopeful but it's nice to think there may be something we can do. They may not teach you proper swearing at school, but they keep your head on straight all right. Good boy.'

In consequence of Mr Baker's visit to the police station, Potter soon received a letter from a firm of solicitors acting for Mr Baker. Potter accordingly went to another firm of solicitors, the usual battle of letters took place and a writ was issued. The dividend which the winning coupon had won was £30,000 and Mr Baker accordingly claimed that he was entitled to £15,000. As Potter was in any event entitled to £15,000, it would have been very sensible of him to offer to split the other £15,000 with Mr Baker. This would have given Mr Baker £7,500, which is quite a tidy sum, and left Potter with £22,500, which is even tidier. The worry and expense of litigation would have been altogether avoided and, as far as Mr Baker was concerned, he would have been very well advised to have accepted such an offer for, while it was £15,000 or £30,000 to Potter, it was £15,000 or nothing for Mr Baker. However, Potter had at least one of the seven deadly sins and the fact that he had £15,000 in any event only strengthened his resolve to resist Mr Baker's claim. Mr Baker, on the other hand, was pretty well fighting for his life as he was as likely or unlikely to win the treble chance pool again as he was of being murdered.

CHAPTER THREE

Consultation

About three months after the dispute arose, Mr Baker's solicitors instructed Culsworth to lead for the Plaintiff, and Mr Baker accordingly had his first consultation with a QC. It was indeed his first visit to the Temple, and he was not particularly impressed with Culsworth's chambers. The main sources of his knowledge of legal procedure were American films and he had expected the luxurious offices which fashionable lawyers usually have, decorated with secretaries and pictures and other expensive furniture. But chambers in the Temple are even today seldom like that. It is true that, when first occupied, Culsworth's chambers had broken with tradition. They had been clean. Moreover they lacked places where dirt could most easily collect. However, after ten years of occupation by Culsworth and the barristers who had gathered round him, and the clerk who had suckled him from the date of his birth into the law, a good deal had been done, if not to put matters right, at any rate to show that the new generation did not wholly despise the habits of its predecessors. By the time Mr Baker called, a good deal of dirt had managed to find a home and the rooms in their untidiness looked more like the chambers of barristers in busy practice than the cold-looking, clean,

14

business-like offices they had resembled when first built. Hitler could break the stones of the Temple but not its spirit.

The two most important people in the chambers were Culsworth and Mr Digby, the clerk. In the pleasantest possible manner they laid down how the chambers should be run, and anyone who disagreed with the rules they prescribed was free to leave on giving three months' notice. This freedom was more theoretical than practical as it was obvious to anyone that the prosperity available with Messrs Culsworth and Digby compared very favourably with that offered by most other sets of chambers. It is difficult to get on at the Bar but, once a person who has the ability to succeed is established in prosperous chambers, he has only minor matters to worry about; such as seeing his wife and children, getting enough sleep and indulging in any of those hobbies in which men in almost every walk of life (except that of the successful barrister) are able to indulge. There was no doubt about it, No. 3 Coleridge Court, oozed prosperity.

Culsworth himself had the usual farm and small house in the country and a flat in London, two cars, two daughters and a wife. Since taking silk he had had more time to spend with his wife and was delighted to find that she was still the kind, attractive woman whom he had married years before and almost forgotten. It presumably shows what outstanding people most successful barristers must be that they do not lose their wives to rich, handsome and idle strangers. But perhaps there are not enough of these to go round, or they get caught hovering round the film studios.

Mr Baker was not interested in Culsworth's private life, only in his professional skill, and he was pleased to find, as soon as the consultation began, that he seemed to know all about his case. He had been told that some lawyers were so busy that, when you called to discuss with them the case of a burst boiler, they treated you for the first half hour as though you were co-respondent in a divorce case, with a very ropy defence indeed.

'So you were in your pyjamas, were you?' they ask you in a hostile manner. 'How are you going to explain that to the judge?'

And it is only after you have explained that you were aroused from sleep by the sound of water pouring through the ceiling that they change their tone and apologise for confusing your case with that of Mr Anstruther. Up till then they have treated you rather like a criminal and refused to let you say a word.

'Now, Mr Blank, before we go thoroughly into the facts of this case I want to explain that my only object is to help you, but that I shan't be able to do that unless you tell me the truth and the whole truth. Now I know that some members of the public think that lawyers are paid to make up stories for their clients. Let me assure you, Mr Blank, that that is not the case in this country and, if you did go to bed with Mrs Smith, the sooner you tell me so the better. No, please don't interrupt. I'll hear everything you have to say in due course. It's quite true that if you do tell me you're guilty I shan't be able to pretend that you're not, but there are still certain things I can do on your behalf which may be much better for you than if I put up the pretty odd story you appear to have told your solicitors. It may be true that you wanted the bicarbonate of soda in the middle of the night, and that it was in Mrs Smith's bedroom, but are you seriously saying that it takes an hour and a half to mix yourself a dose of bicarbonate of soda and water? No, I quite follow. Mrs Smith woke up and you started chatting to her. About what, may I ask, at two o'clock in the morning? And did you take the bicarbonate of soda before or after the chat? And how is it, pray, that the packet of bicarbonate of soda was found new and unopened in the morning? Was your chat with Mrs Smith so exhilarating that it drove your indigestion away or made you forget it? If so, I should be failing in my duty to you if I did not point out that that is not far removed from what your opponent is going to say, only he will suggest that you had rather more than a chat. Rather more than a chat, I said. Well, did you, Mr Blank? Did you have rather more than a chat? Now you know quite well what I mean. If Mrs Smith attracted you when you were playing tennis with her, and punting her down the river – no, they're making no allegation about that incident as they haven't any evidence – it was a gramophone you took with you, not a recording machine – fortunately, if I may say so – if she attracted you on those occasions did she not attract you when she was in bed? Or were you concentrating entirely on the bicarbonate of soda – the packet of which you did not even open? Or are you saying you finished up the remains of an old packet – and I'm not referring to Mrs Smith – and threw it away in the wastepaper basket? If so, strange that the person who emptied the contents of that basket says there was no such empty packet in it. Oh yes, the person may have been bribed by the other side to say so. But, before I make allegations of that kind, there's got to be some evidence about it. I am not prepared to make charges of that sort without some justification. And another point. As there was no glass and no water in Mrs Smith's bedroom, how did you mix it there? Why didn't you just go in, apologise for awakening Mrs Smith – if she was not already wide awake and waiting for you – I said waiting for you, Mr Blank – apologise, take the bicarbonate and leave Mrs Smith to continue her innocent slumbers? Mr Blank, I'm your counsel and I will, if you insist, continue to put up this cock and bull story on your behalf with all the skill I possess, but don't think you'll get away with it. If I don't believe it, who d'you think will? I'm on your side, you pay me, and if *I* think you're a low, yellow-bellied twister, what d'you think the other side – the people whom you don't pay – who hate your guts – what d'you think they're going to say about you? I could tell you what I'd say if I were in their shoes.'

But the consultation with Culsworth was not on these lines at all. He had read the papers, he did not confuse them with any others and he only asked Mr Baker questions directly concerning the matter. Before he left, Mr Baker asked Culsworth what were his chances of winning.

'Well, as you realise, it's word against word, so that pretty well everything will depend upon how each of you gives his evidence. It's a pity you didn't go to see him with a friend before you went to a solicitor. He might have said something which helped, even though he denied his liability. However, we must do the best we can with what we've got. You've at least a fifty-fifty chance. To some extent it depends upon the judge. There are some judges who think a man wouldn't bring a case unless he knew he was in the right. There are others who think a man wouldn't defend a case unless *he* knew he was in the right.'

'Well, choose the right one,' said Mr Baker.

'I'm afraid we can't choose our judges,' said Culsworth.

'If we could,' he added later on to his junior after Mr Baker had left, 'there are one or two who wouldn't have any cases to try at all.'

CHAPTER FOUR

Mr Sampson

Culsworth's junior and solicitor remained with him at the end of the consultation, to discuss another matter, and Mr Baker left the room alone. Before leaving the chambers he had a short chat with a clerk.

'Strange place,' he said. 'Never knew it existed. So quiet like. Are they all lawyers here?'

'Oh no,' said the clerk, 'not necessarily. There are some residential chambers, and you may find anyone there. Usually it's a lawyer, but take upstairs, for example. They're nothing to do with the law.'

Above Culsworth's chambers there had lived for about six months a married couple called Edward and Margaret Verney. Margaret was a particularly attractive woman of thirty-five and her husband seemed an easy-going friendly person. He appeared to spend a good deal of his time travelling and was seldom seen by the members of Culsworth's chambers. Margaret, on the other hand, had got to know Culsworth fairly well. It started when the electricity failed and she made tea for the whole of his chambers. After that he used sometimes to go up for a drink before going home. Only on one of these occasions was Edward Verney present, but there was nothing even faintly improper in Margaret's association with Culsworth. Just a pleasant interlude on his way home.

One morning, while her husband was out, a man knocked at the Verneys' door. Margaret opened it.

'My name is Sampson,' said the man. 'You won't know me, but I wonder if I might have a word with you?'

He was quite well dressed and had a pleasant voice and appearance. Margaret invited him into the sitting room.

'Nice place you have here,' he said. 'And what a lovely view. Your husband home?'

'How did you know I was married?'

'So he's out.'

'Really, Mr – Mr ...'

'Sampson – shouldn't be too difficult to remember, though I have quite a number of namesakes. Not related, though. Verney's a much less common name.'

'Mr Sampson,' said Margaret, 'would you kindly tell me why you wish to see me?'

'I'm sorry. I'm rather inclined to digress in pleasant company. I hate work. An informal chat is so much more pleasant.'

'If it's insurance,' said Margaret, 'I'm afraid we have all we want.'

'How can you be so certain?' said the man. 'You don't know what I have to offer.'

'Then it is insurance?'

'In a way, yes.'

Margaret got up.

'I'm extremely sorry,' she said. 'I know how depressing it must be for you, but I assure you we have no spare funds to take out another policy, even if we wanted to.'

'No spare funds, you say. Well, that all depends, doesn't it? You don't know how much you need the insurance. We all have spare funds, however poor we are. If you really need one thing you can give up another. If drink is necessary for you, you can give up smoking. If you don't drink or smoke you can give up buying the paper or you can eat less. Even people on the bread line can eat less bread if there's something they need more. And looking around this charming flat in these charming surroundings I should hardly say you were on the bread line. No, Mrs Verney, you have plenty of spare funds if you need them.'

'I don't know why I should tell you this,' said Margaret, 'as I must say I find your behaviour rather extraordinary, but in point of fact we are at the moment extremely short of money.'

'Hard up, you'd say?'

'Yes.'

'Well, so am I.'

'I'm sorry,' said Margaret, 'and, as a matter of fact, I do know what it means to make fruitless calls from house to house, but I'm afraid I can't help you.'

'But you're wrong. You can. You've got no idea what a person can do if he really needs something. Or if *she* really needs something either.'

'There are plenty of things we'd like to have, if we could afford them and, if we had the money, I'm afraid they'd come before insurance.'

'Of course. I'm not talking about things you'd like to have. I'm talking about things you've *got* to have. How many Verneys would you say there are in the British Isles?'

'I've no idea, and what's that got to do with it?'

'If a hundred pounds would save your life you could find it, couldn't you?'

'There's no point in discussing the matter. I've said all I have to say.'

'But if it would save your life, you could find it, couldn't you? Anyone in your position could. Anyone in any

21

position could find something ... from a penny to a million pounds. We've all got something we would do without to save our lives. People even risk their bodies to save their lives – jumping out of burning houses, for instance.'

'Good morning, Mr Sampson. I'm afraid I've quite a lot to do here and I can't spare you any more time.'

Mr Sampson remained seated.

'I'm afraid I haven't made myself clear,' he said.

'I thought I had,' said Margaret, 'but, as apparently I haven't would you please go?'

'You haven't such a thing as a cigarette, have you?'

Margaret went to the telephone.

'I hate scenes,' she said, 'but unless you leave at once I shall telephone for someone to put you out.'

'I'm sure you wouldn't talk like that if your house were alight and a fireman climbed up a ladder and offered to carry you down.'

'Are you going?'

'I'm the fireman. Please don't get burned alive. Your husband would be most distressed. And I'm sure you'd hate to hurt him. Wonderful thing a happy marriage. Don't spoil it. There are not so many of them. How did you like the Fisherman's Nook Hotel?'

'What did you say?'

'Pretty little place. The room overlooking the lake is the best. Got a private bathroom too. Will your husband be long, d'you think? Perhaps after all I won't wait for him. Don't tell him I called. We'll keep it as a surprise, shall we? I'll come and see you again in a day or two. See if I can interest you in one of my policies. Good morning, Mrs Verney. Sampson's the name, in case you forget. No, don't bother to see me out.'

CHAPTER FIVE

Mr Baker's Case

It was not many days after the man calling himself
Sampson visited Margaret Verney that Mr Baker's case
came on for trial. He had had a further consultation with
Culsworth a week or so beforehand and he was relieved
that the case was to be heard at last. There had been no
unreasonable delay but with so much at stake the days
had dragged horribly. But at last the waiting was over and
Mr Baker heard Culsworth open the case to Mr Justice
Spink with some confidence for, after all, if counsel can't
make his client's case look a good one at the beginning it
would have to be a pretty bad one.

After completing his speech Culsworth called Mr Baker
to give evidence. He told his story quite well and was
eventually cross-examined by Potter's counsel, Andrew
Hopkins. During the course of this cross-examination
Culsworth was surprised to hear Mr Baker say that, after
litigation had started, he had happened to meet Potter in
a public house and Potter, under the influence of drink,
had started to taunt him.

'You'll never win,' he had said. 'My word's as good as
yours. What if I did agree to share it with you? I can
change my mind, can't I? And I did. So there. No one saw

you pay me your share of the stake. So how are you going to prove it, old man?'

'Are you saying that in effect my client admitted to you that he had agreed to go in for the pool with you?'

'He did,' said Mr Baker.

'And when did you first tell anyone that my client made this admission,' asked Hopkins.

'When did I first tell anyone?'

'That's right.'

'How should I know the date? Don't keep a diary like some of you blokes.'

'Don't be rude to counsel,' said the judge.

'Sorry, my Lord, but I'm just an ordinary chap what does his best to earn an honest living, and he seems to want to make out I'm telling a pack of lies.'

'No one's trying to make out you're telling a pack of lies,' said the judge. 'You're just being asked a very simple question.'

'Simple, eh?' said the witness. 'I bet he couldn't tell me when he last saw his grandmother.'

'Behave yourself,' said the judge. 'No one expects you to be able to say the exact date.'

'Then why did he ask it, my Lord?' said Mr Baker.

'I didn't ask the exact date,' said Hopkins.

'You said "when," didn't you?' said Mr Baker, 'and if that ain't asking me the date I don't know what it is. I'm sorry if I'm difficult, my Lord, but I'm no scholar and not used to these places.'

'I didn't ask the *exact* date,' repeated Hopkins.

'Well, you asked the date, and what's the difference? If it was on the 12th and I said the 13th you'd be on me like a ton of bricks – two tons. And I'd get no compensation either. Act of God you'd call it, or such like.'

'Pull yourself together, Mr Baker,' said the judge. 'No one's worrying about a date or an exact date. All Mr Hopkins wants to know is *about* when you told someone else of the defendant's admission.'

'Well, if that's all he wants, why didn't he say so?' complained Mr Baker. 'But I suppose I ought to know. I'm in the Law Courts where things don't mean what they sound like. He asks me when I told anyone and when I says I don't know the date, he tells me he don't want to know it. Might just as well ask me how's your father? Well, I can answer that all right. Ain't got one. Now I suppose he'll say that's impossible. Well, all I can say is – find him, then. I can't.'

'Mr Baker,' said the judge, 'you may be enjoying yourself in the witness box …'

'I like that,' said Mr Baker, 'enjoying meself. I never wanted to come here!'

'Don't interrupt,' said the judge. 'I'm not going to allow you to play the fool any more. Anyway, if you didn't want to come here why did you sue the defendant?'

'Because he wouldn't pay, my Lord. If he'd paid I wouldn't have had to come here.'

'He says he doesn't owe the money.'

'Course he does. He's a liar.'

'Well, then, if *he's* a liar,' said the judge, 'just you tell me about when – within a week or two, a month or two if you like, when did you tell anyone, anyone at all, about the defendant's admission?'

'Well, I don't know, and that's flat,' said Mr Baker. 'I've come here to tell the truth and, if that's what you want, that's all I can say. If you'd like me to make up a date, I can do that all right. Let's say a week last Tuesday.'

'Are you being funny?' asked the judge.

25

'No, my Lord. Come to think of it – it *was* a week last Tuesday.'

'Why didn't you say so before?'

'I forgot. You got me all tied up, like. Couldn't tell if today was Thursday or Christmas.'

'It's Wednesday, as a matter of fact,' said Hopkins.

'There you are,' said Mr Baker triumphantly. 'What did I say!'

'Anyway,' said Hopkins, 'you know that last Tuesday week you told someone of the defendant's admission?'

'Well, what of it?' asked Mr Baker.

'Whom did you tell?'

'Whom did I tell?'

'That was the question.'

'Why should I tell him, my Lord? Can't one have anything private?'

'Whom did you tell?' said the judge.

'Well, if you want to know,' said Mr Baker, 'it was him,' and he pointed to Culsworth.

'I don't want to know what you said,' said Hopkins, 'but you are telling the learned judge, are you, that you told my friend, Mr Culsworth, of this alleged admission by the defendant?'

'You don't want to know what I said!' said Mr Baker. 'Haven't I just told you?'

Culsworth spoke to the solicitor instructing him, and then got up.

'I'm afraid,' he said, 'that I must tell your Lordship that neither my instructing solicitor nor I know anything of this matter.'

'Here,' said Mr Baker angrily, 'whose side are you on?'

'Although Mr Culsworth is representing you,' said the judge, 'it is no part of his duty to corroborate a lie.'

'Who said it's a lie?' said Mr Baker.

'That is for me to judge.'

'Well, *I* say it's true. True as I'm standing here. Why take his word instead of mine?'

'Is there any possibility of mistake, Mr Culsworth?'

'None I'm afraid, my Lord.'

'Well, I say the whole blooming thing's a mistake,' said Mr Baker. 'Suppose it was a lie – it wasn't, but just suppose it was – who's he to give me away? Two hundred pound I've paid him. And what's he do? Tells the judge I'm a liar. Here's fine goings on. "In this case, m'lud, I appear for my client who's a stinking liar." Well, *I* say it's all a stinking shame.'

'Mr Baker, control yourself,' said the judge. 'I will not allow that sort of language in this Court. If you don't immediately apologise I shall deal with you for contempt of Court.'

'I'm sorry, my Lord,' said Mr Baker, 'but can't you see it from my point of view? I pay this 'ere bloke to speak up for me and all he does is sell me down the line.'

'Mr Baker, you will not refer to learned counsel in that way. He is only doing his duty. You should know that in this country barristers and solicitors have a duty towards the Court, as well as towards their clients, and they almost invariably discharge that duty with complete integrity.'

'That's all very fine, my Lord,' said Mr Baker, 'but who's to say who's right and who's wrong? I've sworn on oath to tell the truth and I've told it. Why believe him instead of me? He hasn't even taken an oath.'

'It is customary to accept the word of counsel.'

'Well, my Lord, there must be some bad lawyers. Why, I read about them in the papers. Suppose it's one of them against me, but you don't know he's one of them, why should I be the one to lose? My word's as good as his.'

'I am completely confident in the integrity of Mr Culsworth,' said the judge. 'He is a barrister of many years' standing and is well known to the Court.'

'I dare say he is, my Lord, but how d'you know he hasn't slipped up this time? How d'you know he deserves what you say about him? Everyone's all right till you find out about him.'

'I'm not going to argue with you any more,' said the judge. 'The question is, Mr Culsworth, what is to be done?'

'My Lord,' said Culsworth, 'I obviously no longer have the confidence of my client and, with your Lordship's leave, I and my learned junior will retire from the case.'

'And what happens to me then?' asked Mr Baker.

'You be quiet,' said the judge. 'It seems to me, Mr Culsworth, that this case will have to be retried before another judge, and the plaintiff will be given an Opportunity of instructing, if he wishes, fresh solicitors and counsel.'

'And what happens to the money I've paid,' squealed Mr Baker. 'Do I get it back?'

'You will have to discuss that with your solicitors,' said the judge.

'And what happens next time, my Lord, when I'm asked the same question, does the next bloke – the next gentleman – retire too? And where do we go from there?'

'What do you say, Mr Hopkins,' asked the judge, ignoring Mr Baker's outburst. 'It's all very unfortunate, but I don't see how this trial can go on now, do you?'

'I see the difficulty, my Lord,' said Hopkins, 'but, whoever is at fault, it is certainly not the defendant and, if your Lordship is ordering the case to be reheard, I ask that the costs of this abortive trial should be paid by the plaintiff in any event.'

'But suppose in the end it turns out that your client does owe the money, would that be fair?' asked the judge.

'With respect, certainly, my Lord. The case would probably have been finished today or tomorrow. The only reason it has to start again is because there's a dispute between the plaintiff and his counsel. Why should the defendant pay anything because of that?'

'What d'you say, Mr Culsworth?' asked the judge.

'Well, my Lord, if I'm retiring from the case it doesn't seem to me that I can properly argue that matter before your Lordship.'

'Well, someone's got to,' said the judge, and looked at Mr Baker.

'I'm the counsel now, am I?' said Mr Baker. 'Well, I'm worth a darn sight more than the two hundred pounds I paid him. A taxi-driver'd be prosecuted if he threw you out before he'd finished the journey, unless his engine failed. *His* engine hasn't failed,' said Mr Baker, looking at Culsworth.

'I've a very good mind to send you to prison,' said the judge, 'for your continued insolence.'

'Might as well, my Lord. P'raps I'd meet a lawyer *there*.'

'Very well,' said the judge. 'You leave me no alternative. I've given you too much grace already. The case will be adjourned and will start again before another judge. I shall leave the question of costs to the judge who tries the case. The plaintiff will go to prison for contempt of Court. Send for the tipstaff.'

'Mr Baker,' said the judge, when the tipstaff had arrived, 'the length of time you spend in prison depends partly upon you. You have behaved quite disgracefully and Courts of Law could not be carried on if conduct such as yours were tolerated. However, if after a fortnight you choose to make a full and proper apology to the Court, I will then consider ordering your release.'

'I may want longer than a fortnight, my Lord,' said Mr Baker. 'There ain't so many lawyers inside as there ought to be. Give me time to wait for him,' and he pointed to Culsworth.

'I will certainly give you a longer time in prison,' said the judge. 'I can see that leniency does not pay in your case. I will consider ordering your release after six months.'

'Thank you, my Lord,' said Mr Baker. 'P'raps you'll be there by then.'

'Take him away,' said the judge, 'before he says any more. I shall now make it twelve months.'

'Take *me* away, before *he* says any more,' said Mr Baker. Mr Baker was accordingly taken away to Brixton, and on the way he expressed his view of the law and lawyers even more freely than he had done in Court. And it was all because of that creep. He quite startled the prison officers with his sudden 'Creep, creep, creep.'

CHAPTER SIX

Unofficial Consultation

The day after Culsworth had refused to act for Mr Baker, Margaret Verney came down to his clerk.

'D'you think it would be possible,' she said, 'for Mr Culsworth to see me for ten minutes some time? It's a personal matter.'

'I'm sure he'd be delighted, Mrs Verney,' said Digby, 'but he's a bit booked up today. Would tomorrow do?'

'Well, of course, if necessary, but it is rather urgent.'

'Well, I'll see what I can do. Just wait a moment.'

Digby went into Culworth's room.

'Mrs Verney from upstairs says she wants to see you rather urgently.'

'Oh?' said Culsworth surprised. 'D'you know what it's about?'

'No idea, but she seems a bit agitated. Shall I keep the Robinson case waiting and let her see you now?'

'All right,' said Culsworth, 'show her in. I wonder what on earth she wants.'

Digby brought Margaret into Culsworth's room and went back to his own.

'I'm awfully sorry to trouble you,' Margaret began.

'That's all right. How can I help?'

'It seems so unfair taking advantage of our living just above you.'

'Not at all. Only too pleased. What's the trouble?'

'Forgive my asking this – but everything I say will be in confidence, won't it?'

'Well, of course – unless you want advice as to how to commit a crime.'

'It certainly isn't that. The other way round, if anything. But you wouldn't mention it, even to my husband?'

'I see,' said Culsworth, and stopped to think for a moment.

'I'm afraid it's embarrassing you,' said Margaret.

'Well, it is a bit embarrassing,' said Culsworth. 'You and your husband both live above us. If there's trouble between you, I shouldn't want to take sides. I'm sure you'll understand that.'

'Of course. No, there isn't exactly trouble between us. It's to prevent it really that I came to see you.'

'All right,' said Culsworth, 'I'll take a chance. I won't tell your husband.'

It was not an easy decision to make, but in the end, whether he fully realised it or not, it was Margaret's attractive appearance which was the decisive factor. It is difficult for an ordinary man to refuse a favour to an attractive stranger, and Margaret was not a stranger.

'It's very good of you,' said Margaret, 'and please believe that I wouldn't have dreamed of bothering you in this embarrassing way if it weren't something really serious. But I'm terrified. I felt I must have help at once. And I think only a lawyer can give it.'

'Well,' said Culsworth, 'tell me.'

Margaret said nothing.

'Come along,' he said, 'I've given you my word.'

'Well – I know it sounds melodramatic, but it's true, I assure you. I'm being blackmailed.'

Culsworth thought for a moment and then said: 'I've a consultation in a few minutes and it's obvious that you can't tell me all about it in that time. Could you come back later?'

'Of course – but – but – how much later?'

'Oh, about 5 o'clock. How would that be?'

'The truth is my husband will be back by then and, until I've told someone about it, I don't see how I can keep it from him. He's bound to see something's wrong. It's all bottled up inside me and I'm bursting to tell you and get help. I know I oughtn't to talk like this – will you forgive me?'

Culsworth picked up the telephone.

'Digby,' he said, when the clerk answered, 'I shall be rather longer with Mrs Verney than I expected. Will you apologise to everyone and say I'll be as quick as I can? Thanks.'

He put down the receiver.

'You are kind,' said Margaret.

'Now, get it off your chest. Perhaps it isn't as bad as you think.'

After a few moments' hesitation, Margaret told him of her interview with Sampson.

'If that's his real name. Heaven knows who he is!'

'And what is it you think he knows?'

'Well, you can guess, I suppose. While Edward was abroad I did make a fool of myself and go to that hotel – and I wasn't alone.'

'A man?'

'Of course.'

The tone of her answer showed slight resentment at the precision required by the lawyer.

'I'm sorry,' she added. 'Naturally you've got to know everything. Only I felt that, if it had been my Aunt Barbara I went with, I shouldn't be asking for help now.'

'I quite understand. Don't upset yourself. And, of course, your husband knows nothing about it?'

This time she appeared to check the resentment which she had shown before.

'No, he doesn't.'

'Well, surely,' said Culsworth, 'that's the simple answer to your problem. Tell him.'

'It isn't, you see. If it had been, I shouldn't have bothered you now.'

'Is he such a jealous person, then?'

'No, not particularly. If I'd told him when he came back from abroad I'm sure it'd have been quite all right. But he was so pleased to see me when he arrived, and so loving, I felt I just couldn't tell him then. You can see that, can't you? He came back carrying loads of flowers and presents – "it's just wonderful to be with you again – d'you know, I've thought of you almost every minute I've been away. Now, tell me all you've been doing." "Well, as a matter of fact, I went away for a weekend with a man." You see, I just couldn't then – and after that I kept putting it off. Now it's too late.'

'I'm sure it isn't. You're a happily married couple, and you say he's not a jealous type. He's sure to forgive you.'

'That would have been the case.'

'Well, why isn't it?'

'The other day he asked *me* to divorce *him*.'

'What! I thought you were so happy together.'

'So we are – and will be, I'm sure. But he's suddenly got an absurd infatuation for a much younger woman. He'll get over it, I know, and of course I'd forgive him. And I wouldn't dream of playing into her hands by divorcing him now. I'm sure he'll see what an idiot he is before long. Of course, if I'm wrong and the affair went on for years I might have to let him go, but I'm sure it won't. And we're so happy – really we are – just as you thought. And once we get this woman out of the way we shall be again. But, if he heard of my weekend now, he'd divorce me. She'd make him.'

'He'd have to get the Court to exercise discretion in his own favour if he's done the same himself.'

'How does that help? First of all, I've no proof at the moment that it's gone as far as that. But, even if it has, doesn't the Court usually exercise its discretion except in very bad cases?'

'Yes, I'm afraid that is so. And you can't say this is a really bad case. After all, your offence came first and you never told him about it.'

'Exactly. So you see, don't you, that I simply can't tell him.'

'I see the difficulty,' said Culsworth. 'Now, let me think what other courses are open to you. You could go to the police, of course.'

'But I can't possibly. Edward would be bound to hear of it. All this Mrs X stuff may be all right for the general public, but I'll bet Mr X usually knows all about it. There'd have to be traps set for the man, wouldn't there? And then I'd have to go to the Courts to give evidence. And we're known in the Temple. Even if no one recognised me, I'd have to explain to Edward where I was, and I couldn't keep making excuses successfully all the time.'

'Yes,' said Culsworth, 'I see that difficulty too. There is another method, but it would mean your paying the man something. Of course, it all depends on how much he thinks it's worth. Could you raise £100?'

'Not without Edward knowing all about it. We've a joint account and I can draw on it, but I'd never be able to draw out as much as that. He'd want to know why and, even if I tried to lie my way out of it, I'd be bound to break down in the end. But how would it help if I did raise £100?'

'Well, you see, if this man agreed not to molest you any more in return for a sum of money, you could get an injunction against him if he broke his word. And if he broke the injunction he'd be sent to prison.'

'But what about the publicity?'

'With luck there wouldn't be any. It could all be done privately. The method isn't bound to be successful, because the man could, if he wanted to, appeal to the Court of Appeal, and, even though he lost the appeal, it would be heard in public and the damage would be done. But that doesn't usually happen, and normally when a blackmailer knows his victim has gone to the Court he gives in. He usually wants money, not revenge, and he doesn't want to go to prison. What's the most you could raise without exciting suspicion?'

'Well – I suppose I might manage £25 over a few weeks, but not a penny more.'

'That's one possibility, then, if he'll take as little. The other thing is to do nothing at all.'

'But then he'll tell Edward.'

'Not necessarily. As I said before, blackmailers normally want money, not revenge. This man is a complete stranger to you. It's highly unlikely that he's any grudge against you. Once he tells your husband he's no hold over you – nothing to sell to you. Of course, I realise it would put you under a dreadful strain all the time.'

'I'll have that anyway until this young woman is out of the way. Once that episode is over I can tell him, and everything will be all right.'

'How d'you think this man knows about your visit to the hotel?'

'I've no idea. He might have been a waiter there. He might somehow have learned about it from Freddie. He's the man I went with. He was very wealthy, and I think he had a valet. Something like that, I imagine.'

'Well, at the moment I think the best thing is to keep on putting him off with excuses. About raising the money, or something. He certainly won't tell your husband while there's any chance of his getting anything from you. Try to find out how much he'll take to make the agreement I mentioned. Then, if you can raise the amount, get him to sign. I'll draft something for you, if you like.'

'That would be most kind.'

Culsworth took a piece of blank paper and wrote for a few minutes.

'Here you are,' he said. 'I think that'll do. After he's signed it, take it to Bush House and get it stamped.'

'And suppose he won't, or suppose I can't find the money he wants?'

'Then we'll have to think again.'

Margaret got up.

'It is kind of you,' she said. 'I feel better already. Now that I've got someone to help me, I can't tell you what it means. I think I'd have gone mad if you hadn't been so good to me. Even now the thought of seeing him again makes me freeze inside. But then I can think of you – and so near, too. I can't tell you how grateful I am.'

She said goodbye, left and went upstairs.

The man was outside her door, about to ring.

'What a piece of luck,' he said. 'I'd have been so disappointed if you'd been out.'

CHAPTER SEVEN

Mr Baker's Contempt

Mr Baker did not like it in Brixton and, at the suggestion of the Governor, he instructed a new solicitor, who came to see him.

'You're in a nice mess,' he said. 'As pretty a kettle of fish as ever I saw.'

The solicitor, Mr Menton, was a small friendly man with sparkling blue eyes, and a mouth and upturned nose for which most comedians would have paid a lot of money. He savoured Mr Baker's case as a connoisseur savours port. It seemed to give him the greatest pleasure and amusement but, just as Mr Baker was about to ask him to take that grin off his face and it was all very well for him to smile he could go out when the interview was over, Mr Menton spoke so encouragingly to his client that his first anger abated at once.

'Well, we must get you out of this,' he said. 'A year in Brixton for cheeking a judge. We can't allow that, can we? Between you and me, there was a lot of good sense in what you said, but you put it the wrong way – and I'm sure that even you will agree that it was tactless to suggest that the old boy would soon be here himself. You'll have to take that part of it back, you know. That *was* rude. We can't justify that. Oh, dear me, no. But I'd have liked to have heard you. I once heard a woman call a judge a big fat bully, but there was no finesse about that. Yours was much neater. I bet there was a gasp in Court and then a hush. I can just imagine all that breath being sucked in suddenly and held there until the audience recovered. Must have made quite a breeze when they came to.'

'I don't know what you're talking about,' said Mr Baker, 'but what did she get?'

'Six months, I think, but I wouldn't be sure. I wasn't in the case. I just happened to be there.'

'But if I get six months that creep will have spent all the money – or hidden it somewhere.'

'Oh – we can still go on with your case.'

'From here?'

'Oh, certainly. They'll let you out as often as need be while it's being tried. All the same, it's not the best way to conduct litigation. A year he said, didn't he? Well, we must get you out long before that. Now, I'll prepare an affidavit for you to swear and we'll apply for your release in the fortnight he first mentioned. My clerk will bring it along in a couple of days. Don't worry about the language. It won't be quite the way you speak, but just see that it's all true before you swear it. That's important.'

Mr Menton got up. 'My, this is a dreary place,' he said. 'We can't let you stay here. My snakes, no!'

'What have snakes got to do with it?' asked Mr Baker. 'Pardon the liberty, but I don't reckon to have heard the expression before.'

'What's wrong with it?' asked Mr Menton. 'Would you prefer "my giddy aunt"? I haven't an aunt and, if I had, it's most unlikely that she'd be giddy. We all use meaningless phrases. Mine's as good as any, isn't it? Takes your mind off the wallpaper. I've used it since I was a boy. Good morning.'

A few days later Mr Baker received a draft of the proposed affidavit. It was indeed written in different language from that normally spoken by him. Lawyers always make their clients swear affidavits in their own language however differently their clients may speak. It would, however, be a refreshing innovation to read something like this: 'I, Albert Smith, of 12 Nosegay Buildings in the County of London East 19, make oath and say as follows:

'1. S'welp me, guv, I don't owe the … a sausage,' instead of the more prosaic:

'1. I deny that I am indebted to the plaintiff in the sum of £100 or any part thereof.'

The words which Mr Menton suggested that Mr Baker should put on oath were as follows: '1. I am the plaintiff in this action which is brought to recover £15,000 from the defendant in the following circumstances.

'2. The defendant and I agreed that we should enter a football pool competition together. We were to share the stake money and any prize or prizes. The coupon was to be sent in the name of the defendant. I suggested two important entries and we did the others together. I paid the defendant half the stake money, namely ten shillings and sixpence, and the defendant sent in the coupon. It won prizes totalling £30,000, but the defendant pretended that we had made no agreement at all and repudiated all liability. He denied that I had paid any of the stake money or helped to fill in the coupon.

'3. Later, after this action had started I happened to meet the defendant in a public house. He in effect admitted my claim but said I'd never be able to prove it.

'4. I told this to my counsel, Mr Culsworth, about a week before the trial, I think on a Tuesday. I had not told him before because I had not considered it important. No one was present when the defendant made the admission and I realised that, if the defendant denied the original agreement, he would obviously deny this subsequent admission. I have never given evidence before in any case and, when I was being cross-examined about this matter, I at first became confused in the witness box and forgot I had told Mr Culsworth about the defendant's admission. Shortly afterwards I remembered that I had told him and said so. To my horror and indignation Mr Culsworth got up and said I had never told him. I realise now that Mr Culsworth no doubt has a lot of cases and might have forgotten the incident or misunderstood what I said, but at the time I became violently indignant at what I considered to be the betrayal by an advocate of his client. I admit that I lost my temper and said things which I ought never to have said. I am rather a quick-tempered man and, once I start getting in a rage, I am inclined to keep it up for quite a long time. In fact I did not on this occasion recover myself until I had been in prison some hours. I felt that every man's hand was against me, that I had been let down by my own counsel to whom I had paid what was, for me, a large sum of money, and that the learned judge was taking counsel's part instead of being completely impartial.

'5. I now realise that I ought never to have behaved as I did, that I ought to have controlled myself, and that I should never have spoken to the learned judge as I did. I am deeply sorry for what I did and I offer my most humble apologies to the Court for my behaviour. My only excuse is that I could see my £15,000 being spirited away from me by what – I thought then – was my counsel's deliberate betrayal of his trust, but which I now realise was due simply to his forgetfulness or to a misunderstanding. It is very rare for anyone to win £15,000 in a football pool or any other competition. It opens up a completely new life for the winner and his family. They can buy a house and a car, and start to enjoy all sorts of amenities (including higher education) that would otherwise be impossible for them. It is a chance which, if it comes to a man at all, is most unlikely to be repeated, and to see all this suddenly being taken away from me through no fault of my own was more than I could bear and I hardly knew what I was doing.

'6. I fully realise that conduct such as mine cannot possibly be tolerated in a Court of Law and I accordingly repeat my humble apologies and promise that I will never behave like that again.

'7. In the above circumstances I humbly ask for my immediate release from prison. I respectfully submit that, as I have never been in prison before, the time I have now spent there, coupled with my appreciation of my offence and my unqualified apologies for it, constitute a purging of my contempt. I would also respectfully point out that I desire to proceed with my action at the earliest possible moment and that it is, at the least, highly inconvenient for a person to conduct litigation from prison.'

Mr Baker read the draft with some little difficulty and later had a further interview with Mr Menton.

'It doesn't matter what I think, so long as I sign?' he asked.

'No,' said Mr Menton, 'you may think what you like, so long as what you say is true.'

'Well, I say I'm sorry, don't I? And I'm not. I think they're a lot of so-and-so's, the judge and all.'

'I don't think it would help to put that in,' said Mr Menton, 'and surely you're sorry you're in prison?'

'Yes, but ...'

'Then you must be sorry that you did something which landed you in prison.'

'I suppose so.'

'Then you're sorry you said what you did.'

'It wouldn't have mattered if I'd thought it, then?'

'My snakes, no!' said Mr Menton. 'Why, even counsel say to a judge "with the greatest possible respect I submit," when all the time they're thinking: "You blithering old idiot, you ought to have got the point years ago".'

'But they don't never say it?'

'No, they don't never say it,' repeated Mr Menton, 'or they'd soon be where you are. One of these days there may be automatic thought-recorders and then we'll have to be most careful. Not much good saying to the judge then: "Your Lordship is always most kind and considerate," when the old boy can see coming up on the old thought-recorder: "You blankety-blank, you're doing this out of pure cussedness." However, that won't come about in my time, I hope. No, you can sign the "sorry" part of it all right, Mr Baker. Everyone does. We're all sorry when we're caught, or in prison.'

'What! Have you been inside?'

'My snakes, no!' said Mr Menton. 'I was just generalising.'

So Mr Baker swore the affidavit and three weeks after he had been sent to prison an application was made to Mr Justice Spink for his release. Against his solicitor's advice Mr Baker made the application himself but Mr Menton was in court to advise him, if necessary.

'I've read your affidavit,' said Mr Justice Spink. 'It's very well worded. How much d'you mean of it?'

Mr Baker looked cautiously at his solicitor, who turned his head slightly away to prevent the judge from thinking that he was prompting his client.

'It's no good looking at Mr Menton,' said the judge. 'He's done his part by drafting an excellent affidavit. What I want to know now is if it's really true – whether you really are sorry. Or did you just sign it because your solicitor said you should?'

Mr Baker remained silent.

'Well, come along,' said the judge. 'First of all, d'you realise that you should never have behaved as you did?'

'I'd want me brains tested if I didn't, my Lord,' said Mr Baker. 'What I did landed me in Brixton.'

'Go back there,' said the judge. 'I don't like your attitude at all.'

After he had been removed, Mr Baker was allowed to have an interview with Mr Menton.

'Short and sharp, I'm afraid,' said Mr Menton. 'I told you it would have been better if counsel had made the application for you. He would have answered the question all right. I'm afraid you weren't very tactful.'

'None of you lawyers want the truth. And the truth is, I think the whole bleeding lot are a bunch of stinking so-and-sos. And if you don't know what I mean by so-and-sos I can tell you. Not you, of course, Mr Menton. You seem all right.'

'Well, that's something,' said Mr Menton. 'Now, what we've got to decide is whether to wait a bit, and try the old boy again, or whether we'll go to the Court of Appeal.'

'What's that?'

'You've a right to appeal against his refusal to let you out.'

'And who hears that? Another of them baskets?'

'Three of them, I'm afraid.'

'Three of them!' said Mr Baker aghast. 'Can they hang me?'

'Oh, dear me, no. The worst thing they can do is to dismiss your appeal and make you pay the costs.'

'Who gets them? The three baskets?'

'Oh dear no. They just get salaries. It doesn't make any difference to them whether they send you back to prison or let you out.'

'Well, if it don't make no difference, they ought to let me out. What d'you think?'

'I'm afraid I just can't say. It's only fairly recently that a man in your position has had a right to appeal. But I think we'll try. I think they may be more sympathetic. But do be a bit tactful, Mr Baker. Say you're sorry, if you can.'

'There you go again. All you lawyers talk about telling the truth, but you don't want me to tell it. You want me to say: "I'm ashamed of myself, my Lord, hanging's too good for me. Have me hung, drawn and quartered, it's what I deserve and I shan't be happy till I get it".'

'Well, will you have counsel to represent you? You'd do far better if you did. And it wouldn't cost an awful lot.'

'You want me to have him so that he can tell lies for me, don't you?'

'Not lies, Mr Baker, the truth put tactfully.'

'That's what I call lies, Mr Menton. Now I ain't really what you would call a religious man, but I have to speak as I feel, I have to live with myself, see, and if I heard meself say some of the stuff in that piece of paper you made me sign it'd make me sick. It didn't seem so bad just signing me name. Anyway, I couldn't understand half of it. But to come out cold-blooded with all that smarmy stuff, in public too. I couldn't do it, Mr Menton. Respectful, humble, apologies! It's all poppycock, Mr Menton. I ain't respectful, I ain't humble, and I don't mean none of them apologies. My counsel *was* a stinker, the judge *was* a stinker. The only person who wasn't too bad actually was the bloke on the other side. After all, he was *paid* to down me. So I don't blame him for trying.'

'Well,' said Mr Menton, 'it'll be interesting to see how the Court of Appeal react to you. And, on reconsideration, I think it'll be best for you to be yourself. Say what you really think. But don't go out of your way to be rude. There can't be any point in that.'

'Depends what they say to me. How would you like to be told to go back to Brixton just like that? Didn't like my attitude! Well, I didn't like his. Nearly told him so. They're too high and mighty, that's what it is. It ain't as if I'd stolen a car, or something like that. Then, like as not, they'd say that, as it was a first offence, I could go away and do it again. Well – they don't actually tell them to do it again, but that's what it comes to. First offence! Whoever gets caught the first time, I'd like to know. But me – I've never done a thing and off I goes to Brixton because I speaks me mind. It's all wrong. They shouldn't be able to do that to you.'

'Well, be as nice to them as you can,' said Mr Menton. 'As a matter of fact, they're not half bad fellows when you get to know them.'

'Not half bad fellows! So long as you bow and scrape, and call them "me Lord" and be ever so humble, they'll treat you almost like a human being. But you tell them what you really think and they lock you up soon as look at you. What's the good of taking an oath to tell the truth, if they won't let you tell it?'

'It should make a very interesting application,' said Mr Menton. 'We'll appeal at once.'

CHAPTER EIGHT

Information Bureau

Mr Sampson did not say much at his second call on Margaret Verney. He enquired after her husband, her health and her finances, and said he would be back again soon. He kept his word, and was more communicative on the third occasion.

'Getting to know each other quite well,' he said. 'You're paler than when I first met you. Hope it's nothing to do with me.'

'If I am, you know it is.'

'Well, let's hope I shan't have to come much more often.'

'Why d'you come at all?'

'Why d'you think?'

'Isn't it obvious?'

'Well, if it's so obvious, why don't you do something about it?'

'How much d'you want to stay away for ever and keep out of our lives?'

'Nothing. I enjoy these visits.'

'I thought you said you hoped you wouldn't have to come much more often.'

'I've changed my mind since then. When you know me better, you'll find I'm like that. I vary the whole time.

Some people find it fascinating. But I can see that it could be annoying. Which d'you find it?'

'I've never thought about the subject.'

'Well, try.'

'I've better things to do.'

'Such as?'

'That's my business.'

'And your husband's?'

'Please leave my husband out of it.'

'If I took my cue from *you*, I would, wouldn't I? He was kept out of the … the … good Heavens, I've forgotten the name of the hotel – the one by the lake. You know – what was the name? I've got it on the tip of my tongue. Do tell me. It's horrible when you can't think of a word. Do put me out of my agony.'

'You know perfectly well. But how do you know?'

'How do I know? That's a question, isn't it? Well, the answer's easy. Might be useful to you one day. You never know. There's an organisation.'

'What d'you mean?'

'It's just like some of the stores or newspapers have an enquiry department. You can ring up and they'll give you the answer to almost everything. Date of the death of William Pitt junior. How to make a chicken curry. When's the last train to Glasgow. You know the idea.'

'I don't understand.'

'Well, there's an organisation which buys and sells information of a different kind. For instance, suppose you were a waitress in an hotel … the – the – I've got it … The Fisherman's Nook, for instance, and you happened to discover a couple staying together who weren't married. You could sell the information to the people I mentioned. Mightn't get much for it. Depends who they were. They'll pay anything, from half-a-crown to a couple of hundred pounds. Even more for something really good. Then, if you're interested in other people's lives, you can buy a piece of information from the organisation. Again, the price depends on what it is you're buying. They get quite a number of lines which are difficult to sell. They'll let them go in bulk for quite a small sum when they've had them on their books long enough. Like selling bad debts in a way. It's all perfectly legal. It's just information bought and sold. Comes in quite handy sometimes. If you see your next door neighbour pinch something from a self-service store, for instance, don't call the police or tell the store. Just sell it to the organisation. They'll want the proof, mind you. No good just *saying* two people stayed at the Fisherman's Nook, unless you can prove it. But it's rather a good idea, don't you think? Wives can make quite a lot of pin money out of it – if they use it right, that is. You've got to know the market. But I take off my hat to the chap who started it. Of course he had to have a bit of capital to buy the first bits of information. But it soon paid off, I'll bet.'

'How much d'you want for this information?'

'You mean about the Fisherman's Nook?'

'Well – if I were interested in it, yes.'

'Let me think. I bought it in a mixed lot. Paid £150. Averaging out, I'd say your little piece cost me about a tenner. Well, I work on a thousand per cent profit. I know it sounds a lot but, you see, some of the stuff is a dead loss. So you've got to pay for the bad with the good. Your arithmetic good enough to work it out? Thousand per cent on ten pounds – not difficult really.'

'I couldn't pay anything like a hundred pounds.'

'What a pity,' said Sampson, 'well, I mustn't waste your time any more. Just in case you change your mind I'll come along again in a week or so. Goodbye for the present.'

A few days later Margaret's husband received a letter.

'I wonder why they sent *me* this?' he said, and handed to Margaret a brochure of the Fisherman's Nook Hotel.

CHAPTER NINE

Mr Baker's Appeal

Although some 6,000 people are sent to prison each year for not paying debts or instalments of debts which a judge believes they could have paid if they'd tried, imprisonment is *otherwise* regarded by the law as a very serious matter. If a case involves the liberty of the subject, all other cases are jostled out of the way to make room for it. For example, when an accused person appeals to a judge from a magistrate's decision refusing bail, his appeal will be heard by the judge, before any other type of business. Similarly, if a man has been sent to prison for contempt of Court, his appeal from the order sending him there will be accelerated. Accordingly it was not long after Mr Justice Spink had refused to order his release that Mr Baker found himself in front of three judges, Lord Justice Grey, Lord Justice Teeming and Lord Justice Crewe. Once again Mr Baker made the application himself.

'I've got a rough and ready way of speaking, my Lords,' he began. 'I haven't had no education to speak of and I hope the Court won't take against me because of that. The judge who sent me down didn't seem to understand me.'

'Well, you told him he ought to be in prison or used words to that effect. He seemed to understand that,' said Lord Justice Crewe.

'I'd done me nut by then,' said Mr Baker, 'and didn't rightly know what I was saying. I never really thought he'd be sent to prison. No such luck. There, I've done it again! Sorry, my Lord.'

'Mr Baker,' said Lord Justice Teeming, 'do you understand that it would be impossible for the law to be properly administered unless the Courts were treated with proper respect? Now you really haven't yet had time or occasion here to "do your nut" – by which I assume you mean to see red and lose your temper – and yet you quite gratuitously say you wish Mr Justice Spink were in jail. Why d'you make a remark like that? It's insulting to the learned judge and it's insulting to us.'

'I haven't said nothing about your Lordships – yet,' said Mr Baker.

'Even now you have to be rude about us. If you're in your right mind, you must see that that sort of conduct can't be tolerated.'

'It's what I feel, my Lord,' said Mr Baker. 'I can't help it, but it wouldn't be true to say I didn't. I do wish the judge were in prison and I know I'll wish the same for all of you if you don't let me out of it. Begging your pardon,' he added.

'Is it necessary to say so publicly, Mr Baker? I dare say that litigants who lose cases may in their disappointment or anger wish the judge who tried the case were run over by an omnibus, but they don't say so.'

'That's what my solicitor said, my Lord. He said I mustn't say what I thought.'

'A pity you didn't take his advice.'

'Well, I took an oath, my Lords, and how can I keep it if I don't say what I really think? I could have told the judge I thought he was the best judge in the world, but it wouldn't have been true. I could have wished him "long life," but I wouldn't have meant it. I wished him in the nick and so I said so.'

'Well, one way or another,' said Lord Justice Crewe, 'you'll have to learn that you can't say so and that, if you do, you'll go to prison for a very long time. You have only been there a month so far, and I gather you don't like it.'

'I do not, my Lord.'

'Then, suppose we let you out, what's going to happen at the trial of your action if you don't agree with what the learned judge or with what counsel may say?'

'Blest if I know,' said Mr Baker.

'You mean you may be rude to the judge and counsel again?'

'It all depends, don't it?' said Mr Baker. 'If I feels like telling them to take a flipping walk, I might say so.'

'Why on earth?' asked Lord Justice Crewe. 'I hope you may consider that this court has treated you with courtesy, but that doesn't mean that we agree with all you say. You don't have to be rude to a person because you don't agree with him.'

'It's all those respects and such like, I don't hold with. Why should you sit there and me sit here? We're all made the same.'

'Now, we're not going to have any political speeches here.'

'I got no politics. You got me wrong,' said Mr Baker. 'I think all these 'ere politicians are as bad as you are. Now I've done it again. You better send me back to Brixton, before I do any worse.'

'If you're quite right in the head,' said Lord Justice Teeming, 'there's no earthly reason why you shouldn't behave like other people. You can think what you like about the Courts and Parliament, about judges and politicians, but you've got to behave yourself. You're just like a stupid child.'

'Oh, I am, am I?' said Mr Baker. 'If it's names we're starting on, I could think of a few.'

'This appeal will be dismissed,' said Lord Justice Grey, after a short consultation with his brethren, 'but, in our view, the appellant ought to be examined by the prison doctor and by a psychiatrist as well.'

'What happens now?' asked Mr Baker.

'You must go back to prison.'

'Is that for ever?'

'No, after a reasonable interval you can apply again for your release.'

'Who to?'

'To Mr Justice Spink.'

'But he just turned me down.'

'In our view quite rightly. The learned judge ought to have fixed a term to your imprisonment but, as he did not, we shall not so do and there is nothing to prevent you from applying to him again.'

'What's the good of that? He won't change his mind. You should have seen the way he looked at me.'

'Take him away,' said Lord Justice Grey.

'He said that too,' Mr Baker had time to say before he was taken away.

He then had another interview with his solicitor. 'You really will have to be guided by me,' said Mr Menton, 'or you'll spend your life in jail. You let me instruct counsel to apply on your behalf and we'll have you out in a jiffy. What's the good of winning your case if you're in Brixton?'

'Then you think I will win it?'

'If you can convince the next judge of your love for the truth, as you have convinced me,' said Mr Menton, 'you will most certainly win it.'

'All right,' said Mr Baker. 'I don't like it, but there ain't much future in the nick. You tell one of them mouthpieces to do the old respects and humble this and that. I won't have to hear him, will I?'

'It may be necessary,' said Mr Menton, 'but I'll try to avoid it.'

CHAPTER TEN

A Call on Culsworth

The same day that the brochure arrived, Margaret went to see Culsworth.

'I'm afraid this is serious,' he said. 'He's turning on the heat. It's very difficult to know how to advise you. Once you yield to this form of pressure he'll be at you again and again. If you don't yield to it, he'll increase the pressure.'

'What d'you think he'll do?'

'Send something else to your husband. Nothing definite enough to give you away, but something to show that he means business. Now, about your husband's *affaire*, how long d'you really think it will last? The point is – can you keep this man at bay until it's over?'

'Who can say? I should think it would be at least three months, but one just can't tell.'

'And he's still too deeply interested for you to be able to risk telling him?'

'Oh, I couldn't possibly at present. He asked me again yesterday if I'd divorce him.'

'Why hasn't he left you?'

'Well, for one thing she won't have him unless there's a divorce. That's *her* way of putting the pressure on. And then I'm sure that unconsciously he doesn't want to burn his boats. Finally, he'd have to go on supporting me and to keep two homes going would be very expensive – and without a divorce he'd be getting nothing in exchange, or very little. I know I make him sound a pretty rotten person, but he isn't really. He's just weak, and he's lost his head.'

'When is the man coming again?'

'He didn't say. He just comes when he thinks he will.'

'Then he might run into your husband?'

'Well, I've told him the times Edward's not at home, and he always keeps well within them.'

'I'm afraid the next thing he'll do will be to start calling perilously close to the time your husband is expected.'

But that was not in fact the next thing Mr Sampson did. The next thing he did was to call on Culsworth's chambers.

'My name is Sampson,' he said to Digby. 'I wonder if it would be possible for me to see Mr Culsworth?'

'Are you a friend of his, sir?' asked Digby.

'No. A stranger, as a matter of fact. But perhaps you'd just ask him if he'd be prepared to see me?'

'Very well, sir. Excuse me.'

Digby went into Culsworth's room.

'There's a man to see you,' he said. 'Says he's a stranger.'

'What does he want?'

'He didn't say.'

'Well – ask him. What name did he give?'

Digby thought for a moment.

'Samuel, or something …' he said.

'Not Sampson, by any chance?' asked Culsworth.

'Yes – that was it. How did you know?'

Culsworth did not answer the question.

'Tell him I can only spare him a few minutes, and show him in, please,' he said.

'Very well, sir,' said Digby, 'but how *did* you guess his name?'

'Never mind,' said Culsworth. 'Show him in.'

A few moments later Mr Sampson came into Culsworth's room, and sat down in a chair before he was asked to do so.

'Nice position you have here,' he said.

'What is it you want to see me about?'

'Such a pleasant view, and so quiet.'

'I'm afraid I haven't very much time.'

'Nor have I, as a matter of fact. Very good of you to see me.'

'Perhaps you'd tell me why you've come?'

'To see you, of course. To see Brian Culsworth, Esq., QC.'

'Why?'

'It's a new experience. I like new experiences.'

Culsworth got up, intending to tell the man to go. Then he thought better of it and went across to a box of cigarettes.

'What about me? I could use one,' said Mr Sampson.

Culsworth decided to offer him one.

'That's very civil of you, before you know why I'm here.'

'Well – why are you?'

'Look,' said Mr Sampson, 'I might answer that question if you'd answer this one. Why did *you* see *me*? I'm a complete stranger to you. I didn't state my business. You probably don't know anyone of my name. You can't usually see anyone in such circumstances. Why did you?'

Culsworth decided that it was undesirable at that stage to refer to Margaret Verney. The man might well know or suspect that she had come for help and might even have seen her come in, but nevertheless, until that was clear, it was better from her point of view that he should not admit it.

'I wanted to know what you wanted.'

'Well, I want to know why you wanted to know what I wanted.'

Culsworth said nothing.

'We seem to have reached an impasse,' said Mr Sampson. 'I'm sorry to have troubled you. But you have got a nice view through that window. At any rate I've seen that. By the way, weren't you in the Moriarty case some years ago? Good afternoon.'

Mr Sampson got up and went out. Culsworth remained sitting. The Moriarty case. Why on earth had the fellow mentioned that? Culsworth began to think hard, and it was not about Margaret Verney.

CHAPTER ELEVEN

A Clear Round

'My Lord,' said Mr Baker's counsel, Mr Panter, to Mr Justice Spink, 'I have an application to make to your Lordship for the release from prison of a man you committed there last June.'

'Not Mr Baker again?' asked the judge.

'Yes, my Lord.'

'Why on earth should I release him? He behaved disgracefully in the first instance and was quite truculent when he applied to me for his release last time. I gather he was no better in the Court of Appeal.'

'I am instructed to offer his unconditional apologies for his behaviour, my Lord.'

'I dare say you are, but I gave him every chance in the first instance and I said I wouldn't listen to an application until he'd been in prison a year. Why should I reduce the period?'

'A year is a very long time, my Lord, for a first offender who has never been in prison before and whose only crime is gross insolence. Your Lordship will see from my use of those words that I am not trying to minimise his behaviour, only to submit that the punishment should not be too severe for such an offence.'

'I would agree with you, Mr Panter, if your client showed the slightest sign of being sorry for what he's done. But, as far as I know, he's only sorry he's in prison.'

'My Lord, his affidavit says ...'

'His affidavit said a lot of excellent things, Mr Panter, but, as soon as I asked him if he meant them, he became truculent. Where is he now?'

'In prison, my Lord.'

'No doubt his advisers thought it would be easier to obtain his release if he stayed there. Has he been medically examined?'

'Yes, my Lord. A report is attached to a further affidavit and in substance says that he is completely sane.'

'Well, then,' said the judge, 'I'm not going to let him out until he comes here himself and satisfies me that he really is sorry for what he's done, and that he won't do it again.'

'I would urge on your Lordship ...' began Mr Panter.

'It's no use, Mr Panter,' the judge interrupted, 'you can file as many affidavits as you like. As far as I am concerned your client will stay in jail until he comes here and apologises – genuinely – in person. The Court of Appeal can let him out before, if they think fit. As far as I am concerned, he'll stay there for life if necessary. In my view, it would be making a mockery of the Courts to do otherwise. If the man were mentally unbalanced, that would be another matter. But he's just obstinate and contumacious. Well, he must learn that other people can be obstinate too. And I'm one of them.'

'But, my Lord ...'

'No, Mr Panter. You must go to the Court of Appeal if you don't agree with my views. I will not hear you any more in the absence of your client. I'm not unreasonable. You can bring him here this afternoon, if you like. One of the cases in my list has been settled, and there's plenty of time to get him here by two o'clock if you want to. Your clients can tell the Governor that I'll be grateful if he'll arrange for the prisoner's attendance. That's all I can do for you.'

So Mr Panter sat down, and he and Mr Menton reluctantly arranged for Mr Baker to attend the Court. At two o'clock the application for his release was renewed.

'Well, Mr Baker,' said the judge, 'I'm told you may want to apologise for your behaviour. Is that correct?'

Mr Baker swallowed and then said, in a somewhat toneless voice, rather like a child reciting: 'Courts of law could not be carried on unless proper respect is shown to them by all concerned.'

'Is that what you think,' asked the judge, 'or have you just learned it by heart?'

'I learned it by heart as well as I could, my Lord, but there's a bit missing somewhere, I think.'

'D'you agree with it, Mr Baker?'

'Yes my Lord,' said Mr Baker, after slight reflection, 'I could go as far as that.' He had jumped the first hurdle, narrowly missing four faults, perhaps, for the last seven words.

'Are you sorry you did not pay proper respect to the Court yourself, Mr Baker?'

The judge had raised the height of the second hurdle, and Mr Baker eyed it with the distaste of a horse about to refuse. But a refusal would certainly have seen him out of the ring. Suddenly he made a decision.

'Yes, my Lord,' he said, and jumped the obstacle cleanly. Not even a tap.

The judge reflected for about half a minute. He was anxious, if he could, to order Mr Baker's release, but at the same time he felt he had a duty to ensure that contempt in the face of the Court was not lightly condoned.

'Will you promise that such a thing will never occur again, Mr Baker?'

This was several inches higher, and the horse in Mr Baker whinnied. To the judge it only sounded like the clearing of a pretty rough throat. Mr Panter and Mr Menton looked at Mr Baker anxiously, and each felt much as the rider of a horse in the novice class must feel when it has done unexpectedly well and comes to the last fence – one which most horses had had no difficulty in jumping cleanly but to which this horse had taken a particular dislike. On such occasions even the talkers, who spoil other people's enjoyment at horse-shows by jabbering to each other incessantly, sometimes let up and keep quiet. So it was on this occasion. Other counsel and their solicitors, witnesses, court officials and ordinary spectators, recognising that the crisis had come, kept absolutely still. Except for Mr Baker's horse's whinnying there was absolute stillness in Court. The faces of everyone, the judge, the people in the body of the Court, the bewigged associate sitting below the judge, were all turned expectantly towards Mr Baker. If he refused, or knocked down the obstacle, it would have been difficult to think that there would have been sufficient control among those present to prevent a groan going up. Their obvious desire that he should surmount it must have communicated itself to Mr Baker. The mass force of the spectators pushed him over it and, to his surprise, he found himself saying: 'Yes, my Lord, I will.'

And anyone in Court who had thought of the show jumping metaphor must in his mind have heard the judge say: 'A clear round for Mr Baker.'

CHAPTER TWELVE

Culsworth's Lapse

The British legal profession maintains among its members
a high standard of integrity. Occasionally solicitors misuse
their clients' monies. The clients will normally lose
nothing as a result of such conduct, as the Law Society has
a fund from which it reimburses them. Barristers, on the
other hand, never have the temptation to dip into their
clients' monies, as they never have them in their
possession. The temptation to which they succumb very
occasionally is to behave improperly in the course of an
action. Such improprieties are nearly always due to
misplaced enthusiasm on behalf of a client. Either
judgment becomes warped or there is a lack of
appreciation of what is demanded of an advocate or there
is a deliberate yielding to the temptation to win a case. It
has been said by a well-known barrister in his brilliant, if
controversial, book *The Advocate's Devil* that nearly all
barristers of long experience have at one time in the course
of their careers done something which was improper. This
is probably an exaggeration, but there have been rare
instances of surprising behaviour by well-known barristers
who would have been expected to know better.

Culsworth was looked upon by judges and his
colleagues as a person of complete integrity who never

departed from the high standards required of him. But even he had – once and once only – departed from those standards and done something which, if discovered, would certainly have resulted in his being reported to the Benchers of his Inn and might have resulted in his being disbarred. In the course of a capital murder case he had told a deliberate lie to the judge and jury. Battling desperately in a very difficult case for a man who, he had convinced himself, might possibly be innocent, he had suddenly been confronted with very much the same situation as arose in Mr Baker's case. His client, Moriarty, was being cross-examined and he, like Mr Baker, was asked when he had first told anyone of a particular incident. It was at a critical stage of the case and Moriarty in desperation had said that he had told Culsworth. If this had been true, Culsworth would earlier on have cross-examined one of the witnesses for the prosecution about the matter, but he had not done so. Rather than let his client down, Culsworth got up and said that the blame was entirely his, that his client had told him of the incident and that he had accidentally failed to cross-examine about the matter. His word was instantly accepted by the judge, who told the jury that the prisoner's statement must be accepted as true in view of what Culsworth had said. So both judge and jury were deliberately deceived by him. But only two people knew of it, so far as Culsworth could tell, Moriarty and he. Moriarty was convicted, in spite of Culsworth's spirited defence, and sentenced to death but, in view of certain mitigating factors, he was not only reprieved but released earlier than usual.

The case had pretty well passed from Culsworth's mind and he had certainly had few sleepless nights as a result of his own conduct. For some days after the case was over he had thought about it a bit, and had tried to justify his behaviour by the nature of the case, but he soon realised that deliberate deceit could not be justified. So he comforted himself with the thought that Moriarty would certainly not tell the authorities about it. Apart from the ingratitude of such a disclosure, it would also be an admission of perjury. Although prosecutions for perjury in such circumstances are pretty well unknown, Moriarty would be most unlikely to know of this. So Culsworth, having decided that he must never do a thing like that again, let himself off with a caution and pretty well dismissed the matter from his mind.

But, as soon as Sampson mentioned the case, it came back to his mind quickly. And he then at once realised that, though Moriarty would not walk into a police station and say what had happened, he might well have boasted to his friends and relations of how well his counsel had stood up for him. Indeed, thought Culsworth, from Moriarty's point of view his counsel was only doing the right thing. The ethics of the legal profession cannot be expected to appeal much to a man who is in danger of being hanged, and Moriarty might well have thought that Culsworth was only doing what an advocate was expected to do. Perhaps Sampson was a jailbird who'd actually met Moriarty in prison. Or he might have met other prisoners who'd been with him. Or perhaps the organisation which Margaret had told him that Sampson had mentioned had somehow acquired the information. But he would only have mentioned the case if he knew of Culsworth's conduct. The man was a blackmailer. What other object could he have in mentioning it? And now what would happen? Would he have to pay the man? He couldn't do that. You can't start paying a man like that. Perhaps he could make an agreement with him, like the one he suggested to Margaret. He could certainly afford to pay a lump sum to stop the thing once and for all. But would it? Sampson might stop coming for more, but the information could be handed to someone else. Should he go to his Benchers and make a full confession? If he'd done it immediately after the case, it mightn't have been so bad, but to do it only when he was being blackmailed wouldn't be so good.

Suddenly he thought of Margaret's case. He was in exactly the same position as she was. If she'd told her husband at the time, it would have been all right. But now it was too late. Why had he ever defended Moriarty? Why had he tried to save the man by telling a deliberate lie? Then he tried to gain comfort from the fact that a good deal of latitude is allowed to counsel in a criminal case, particularly a murder trial, and this was capital murder. He had had to make a snap decision. He made the wrong one. Admittedly he shouldn't have done it, but was it so very bad at a critical stage of the proceedings? He certainly couldn't have been expected to get up and say that his client was lying. No one would have expected him to throw up the case in the middle. He had just gone too far. In the fury of the battle he had been guilty of a serious indiscretion. Nothing more. But was it nothing more? He had got up and told the judge that Moriarty had told him of the incident. He had heard the judge repeat this to the jury as plainly being true. Was that just indiscreet enthusiasm for a cause?

Then another thought occurred to him. Suppose he refused to be blackmailed. Suppose he told Sampson to do his worst, and suppose the man did report him? If he said that what he had said was true, they would have to believe him. The only word against him would be that of Moriarty himself, who would be admitting perjury. The

Benchers couldn't possibly convict him if he lied again. They might have some suspicions but they couldn't possibly be satisfied on the evidence of Moriarty alone. Indeed, when the blackmail was disclosed, he could probably convince some of the Benchers that these criminals had just thought of an easy way of trying to make money. On the other hand, would they have thought it easy if the allegation hadn't been true? No, the probability would be that most of the Benchers would suspect that there was something in it, but none of them could conceivably convict him if he stuck to his story. But could he? Could he lie again? If he did, his career would be unaffected. If he didn't, he might be ruined. He had not only himself but his wife and children to consider. Was it fair to them to admit his conduct?

Then another thing occurred to him. Was he assuming too easily that, if he lied again, he wouldn't be convicted? There was the undoubted fact that at Moriarty's trial he had failed to cross-examine about the particular incident. That was a very odd thing for experienced counsel to have done. Very odd indeed. It would be a strange coincidence if Moriarty were lying now. So perhaps he would be convicted if he lied again. Anyway, how could he consider coming before his Benchers and deliberately telling lies? That was an impossible thought. He must have been desperate even to have considered it.

His clerk came in: 'I've a message from Donaldson and McBean that they want to call you for the defence in that case of Baker where you threw up the brief. They say they expect you'd prefer to have a subpoena. I said I'd ask you.'

Culsworth did not reply.

'You remember the case, sir? The man who went to prison for contempt. The chap who said he'd told you about the defendant's admission, when he hadn't.'

'Yes,' said Culsworth slowly, 'I remember.'

'Well, the defendant wants you as a witness. There'll be questions of privilege, I suppose, but you'll have to be there, I imagine.'

'Yes, I suppose so,' said Culsworth.

'Will you want a subpoena? I said I thought you would. You can't very well give evidence against your own client voluntarily.'

'Digby,' said Culsworth, 'd'you think that man who called on me – Sampson his name was – d'you think he can be mixed up in that case at all?'

'How should I know, sir? I don't know anything about the man. You just told me to show him in when you heard his name. Are you feeling all right, sir?'

CHAPTER THIRTEEN

A Feminine Point of View

Culsworth was indeed upset. In fact that was a mild word. If he had not known of the blackmailing attempt being made on Margaret, he might have been worried enough, but, knowing what was happening to her, he realised that it could only be days, or at most weeks, before he was in the same position himself. And who could he go to for help? He would not like to have to admit what he had done in the Moriarty case even to one of his intimate friends. He even felt awkward at the idea of telling his wife. But, just as Margaret had said that she was bursting to tell someone, so he knew that it would at least be some help if he could discuss the matter with someone.

But who was there? His clerk? Certainly not. That wouldn't do at all. Someone in chambers? The man who could probably give the best advice was German by origin and he shrank from confiding in a man whom he still looked on as a foreigner. Moreover, he remembered having a discussion with him on the standard of integrity at the English Bar as compared with that in foreign countries. Grumbach had said: 'It is excellent in theory. I wonder how often people don't live up to it.'

'Very rarely indeed,' he had replied. 'And then only in the case of the less reputable chaps. And they're very few.'

No, he certainly couldn't discuss it with him. He knew one of the Law Officers well, but he was a Bencher of his Inn and it would be unfair to embarrass him with it. He could, of course, ask the question theoretically, or as if it related to somebody else, but he felt that would be a very unsatisfactory way of doing it. He thought again of his wife. She was an understanding person. But what would she be able to suggest? And he admitted quite frankly to himself that he hated the idea of admitting to her what he had done. It looked as though he would have to keep the matter to himself. Or should he go straight off to the Director of Public Prosecutions, have a trap laid, and prosecute the man? But that would raise the problem of what he was to say in the witness box. He would either have to commit perjury or admit what he had done.

In the end he decided he must tell his wife. He could not go on alone. Better to hurt his own pride than reduce himself to a nervous wreck by carrying the strain entirely himself.

Jane Culsworth was an ordinary person in the best sense of that word. She had normal likes and dislikes, lost her temper occasionally but only occasionally, and was as unlikely a candidate for the psychiatrist's waiting room as any husband could possibly want. And she adored her husband and was proud of him. Again, not absurdly so. Both she and Culsworth looked down on those wives who always talked about their husbands as though they never lost cases, never made mistakes, and were obviously head and shoulders above all their colleagues. Jane knew her husband was able and likely to go far, but she never assumed, let alone said to other people, that he would go farther than anyone else. She never expected him to be Lord Chancellor or Lord Chief Justice. A High Court judge perhaps, but no more, and only perhaps.

He tried to tell her as soon as he came home. They were settled in chairs having a glass of sherry each.

'Jane,' he said, 'there's something I want to tell you.' He spoke seriously but not so seriously as to convey the full importance of the matter.

'Yes?' she said, quite lightly. 'Just a moment. I must go and look in the oven.'

And she left the room. He cursed. It was going to be difficult to tell her anyway, and now, when he'd got ready to do it, she had to go and look at a beastly joint or whatever it was. Surely it could have waited. She came back in a few minutes.

'Lucky I went,' she said. 'It would have been quite ruined. I was just in time. Oh, by the way, when we have the Lushingtons to dinner, d'you think we should have ... I'm sorry, there was something you wanted to say ...'

'It'll keep,' he said. 'Let's discuss the dinner for the Lushingtons.'

'But that's of no importance. You sounded serious.'

'It doesn't matter.'

He knew that he was behaving rather like a child, but when it comes to matters of pride there is little difference between the behaviour of adults, adolescents and children.

So they discussed the dinner for the Lushingtons in full. The first course, the second course, then should it be a sweet or savoury, or both?

'You should say pudding, not sweet,' she said, 'I've just been reading about it.'

'I'll say nothing of the kind,' he replied. 'To call stewed fruit a pudding is an abuse of language. A roly-poly's a different matter. Anyway, I refuse to be typed as U or non-U. I'll be W if I like. Now, what shall we drink?'

'Are you sure you wouldn't like to tell me what it was you were going to say? The Lushingtons can really wait. They aren't coming for ten days.'

'All right,' he said, 'I will. I'm in the hell of a mess, and I don't know what to do.'

'Not a woman?'

'I wish it were, even if you don't.'

'You sound dreadfully serious.'

'I am. I just don't know what to do. I don't know what I ought to do and I don't know the best thing to do from my own point of view, from our point of view.'

'Then I'm in it too?'

'Only because I am. I'm going to be blackmailed.'

'Blackmailed! But it's impossible. If there isn't a woman in it ...'

'Oh, darling – there never has been one and there isn't one now.'

Jane accepted his denial at once. She was ordinary in being ready to be jealous and ordinary in knowing when her husband was telling the truth.

'But you've done nothing in your life to be blackmailed for. You haven't gone shoplifting have you, or knocked somebody down in a car?'

'No, it's not that. It's something I did in a case. Someone's found out and is going to put the screw on me.'

'But what did you do?'

He told her.

'But you're not being serious?' she said.

'I am. I know it was a very wrong thing to do, but I definitely did it. I'm not trying to excuse myself when I say ...'

'Excuse yourself! What for? When I said you're not being serious I meant that you couldn't think anyone was blackmailing you for that. It's ludicrous. If it wasn't actually your duty to tell a lie, it's only what most lawyers would have done.'

'They wouldn't, I assure you, and they most certainly shouldn't.'

'Suppose your client had been hanged because you'd let him down by telling the truth? That's something which *should* have worried you for the rest of your life, even if you couldn't be blackmailed for it.'

'It wouldn't have worried me in the least.'

'Well it should have then. You seem to worry far more about the rules of your silly profession than about what happens to your wretched clients. They can hang all right, can they, so long as you and your fellow barristers and all the judges can stick to the old school rules and drink the old school port?'

'You don't understand, darling. The reason that lawyers have such a good reputation in this country is because they don't do the things which foreign films make lawyers do.'

'All right. The standard's a high one. Jolly good. But what does it matter if you fall below it once in a way? And how on earth can a man blackmail you for it? I know what I'd say to him. He could tell the world if he liked. He'd get nothing out of me. And the world would hardly read it or listen to it, and those that did wouldn't take the slightest notice.'

'You're quite wrong, really you are. Whatever people outside the profession will say or think, I assure you that the Benchers of my Inn would take a very serious view of the matter indeed, if I admitted it. They'd either disbar or suspend me. Either would mean ruin.'

'Well, that's simple then. Don't admit it. If those stupid old fools would make such a fuss about something which happened years ago, don't tell them. Let them enjoy their port and get on with something that matters.'

'I don't have to go and tell them, though morally I suppose I ought to. But if this chap brings the thing out into the open, or that's the only way I can resist him, I'm bound to be asked if there's any truth in it. And I just couldn't deny it.'

'But, Brian dear, you've been at the Bar for a good many years, haven't you?'

'Yes, of course.'

'And during that time you've done all you could to what you would call, I suppose, uphold the traditions of the Bar?'

'Apart from this affair I suppose I can say that.'

'Then on one occasion you forgot yourself and made a mistake. Did it affect how the case went?'

'Well, no, as a matter of fact, but that was my object.'

'Never mind your object. You didn't cause a miscarriage of justice.'

'No, I certainly didn't. The fellow was convicted. At the time I thought he might be innocent, but I don't any longer.'

'Then what harm have you done?'

'I lied to the Court and was believed. I've never disclosed the truth and I've been allowed to practise ever since.'

'Well, that's done a lot of good. You're above the average, aren't you?'

'Perhaps I am.'

'Then I really don't see what you want to get into a state for. Everyone of us makes mistakes, bad ones sometimes. I've never stolen anything but suppose twenty years ago I took something from a shop. Should I own up now and bring disgrace on all of you? Of course not. I could give the price to the present owners of the business, or to a charity anonymously, but what good would owning up do to anyone except my own silly pride? You've got to think of other people besides yourself – me and the girls for example. And I'm not just being selfish when I say that. What right have you to chuck your whole career away just to satisfy your own conscience? What other person in the world would it benefit, except you?'

'It wouldn't benefit me at all. It would ruin me.'

'Now you're talking like a woman, darling. I ought to know. You would prefer to be ruined with all that it meant to you and us rather than live with a lie round your conscience.'

'But I wouldn't. I've lived with that lie for years and managed pretty well, I should say.'

'Then why not another?'

'That would be different. What I did was inexcusable, but at least it was in the heat of the moment and mainly for my client's benefit. To lie now would be in cold blood and solely to save my own skin.'

'And ours.'

'Yes, to save myself and those I love.'

'Well, I ask you again. What harm would it do to anyone, except you? And, as you were responsible in the first instance, it's only fair that you should be the person to suffer.'

'It would also be a step towards lowering the standard at the Bar. The fact that I was responsible for the first step doesn't entitle me to take another. On the contrary, if I haven't the guts to admit what I did without it being necessary – and I confess I haven't – I simply can't lie again, if I am asked about the matter.'

'Well, however you put it, I think you're just wanting to pander to your own conscience. Anyway, what's going to happen? Why need you be asked about it?'

'I just don't know what's going to happen. I can only guess. This man is quite definitely a blackmailer. He's blackmailing the woman above our chambers, and now he's started on me. If I pay him he'll come back for more and more. And I can't very well make one of those anti-blackmail agreements which ordinary people can make, because I'd have to have my own solicitors and counsel and I'm damned if I'll tell anyone else about it.'

'I thought you were going to confess to your Benchers.'

'If it comes to a showdown, yes, I must. But I absolutely refuse to confide in anyone except you.'

'Suppose you don't pay him? Suppose you just tell him to go to hell?'

'Then I suppose he'll start turning the screw and, if I still refuse to pay, he may turn it so hard that the information leaks out and is enquired into.'

'That'd be no good to him.'

'I know, but he mightn't be able to prevent it. That's what he's doing with the wretched woman upstairs. He knows something she doesn't want her husband to know. Well, gradually he's starting to alert the husband. If she still refuses to pay, he may go too far and the husband will learn about it. That'll be no good to the blackmailer but it'll be fatal for the woman. She's in a spot, and so am I. By Jove!'

'What is it?'

'I suppose I might try to persuade her to prosecute. If they trap the fellow, and he's well and truly in jail for years, that'll stop his fun and games as far as I'm concerned. I can't prosecute, because people in the legal profession would hear about it, but the same considerations don't apply to her.'

'Then why haven't you advised her to do it before?'

'She's frightened that, if there were a prosecution, somehow or other her husband would find out about it.'

'And is that likely?'

'It's possible.'

'So your suggestion is that she should prosecute, with the possibility that her husband will find out, in order to save you. Is that it?'

'I'm afraid it was. I can see it doesn't sound so good.'

'But you'd prefer to do that rather than go straight to your Benchers now and say that an attempt is being made to blackmail you and that there's no truth whatever in the allegations against you?'

'That wouldn't help the woman.'

'Why not? If you did that, the man could be trapped and prosecuted and she'd be in the happy position you hoped to be in if she prosecuted.'

'But I'd have to go into the witness box and commit perjury.'

'Well, you've done that already.'

'No, I haven't. What I said wasn't on oath.'

'You mean barristers only have to tell the truth when they're on oath?'

'No, I don't – but you've got something there. Our simple word is accepted by a judge automatically. That's what makes what I did so bad. But, if I first lie to my Benchers and then lie in the witness box, I don't very well see how I can carry on. And that brings me to another thing I'm worried about. A little while ago I threw up a case in the middle because my client told a lie. Yes, I know what you're going to say. I've become a bit touchy. Well, it was my duty to do it, but you're quite right, since that lie

I told I have been especially meticulous about my behaviour, over-meticulous, if you like.'

'But how does all this come in?'

'Well, I'm being subpoenaed to give evidence for the other side. Now it's an odd coincidence that this should happen just at the time this fellow – he calls himself Sampson – should start on me. There's an organisation of some sort behind him. Suppose the two things are linked up together, I could be cross-examined by the other side about the Moriarty affair. Counsel wouldn't like doing it, but, if it comes to a battle of word against word, he'd be bound to put it to me if he were instructed to do so. If that happens, either I'd have to commit perjury or tell the truth. If I told the truth the Benchers would be forced to enquire into the matter.'

'And if you lied?'

'I'd be all right.'

'When'll you know if this is going to happen?'

'Not until I'm actually in the witness box. That's what's so terrifying. What am I to do, Jane?'

'Well, you know what my advice is. Don't go out of your way to lie but, if necessary, lie your head off. I'll share the blame with you and, I assure you, it won't keep me awake. It won't be nice, of course, but, once it's over, you can get on with your work and forget it.'

'You make it all sound so easy, but I just couldn't do it. I'm sorry I've let you down so.'

'Don't be silly, darling. And, whatever you do, I shan't complain. I believe in complaining before it's too late. That's why I've been trying to hammer my views into you now. But, once you've made the decision, I shan't grumble. Even if we have to go abroad or whatever.'

CHAPTER FOURTEEN

Mr Baker in Conference

It was about the same time as Culsworth and his wife were discussing their problem that Panter was holding a conference with Mr Baker, now happily released from Prison, and Mr Menton. Mr Baker had asked Panter what would happen if the defendant called Culsworth as a witness to refute his statement that he had told him of the defendant's admission.

'Well,' said Panter, 'I think it wisest not to rely upon any technical right you may have as regards your conversation with him.'

'That means as much to me as the top of Nelson's column. Less. I can see that from below.'

'The situation is this,' explained Panter. 'A conversation between a barrister and his client is privileged.'

'Nelson's column,' repeated Mr Baker.

'That means,' went on Panter, 'that without your consent Mr Culsworth would not be allowed to give evidence of what you said.'

'But he said I didn't say nothing. Couldn't he say that?'

'That's a nice point,' said Panter, 'but, whatever the correct answer is, I think we should allow the whole conversation in and I shall cross-examine Mr Culsworth to try and prove it was a mistake.'

'Mistake!' said Mr Baker. 'There wasn't no mistake. He was paid by that so-and-so to do me down.'

'I can assure you that nothing of the sort happened. In the first place no barrister of any kind would dream of doing a thing like that. Secondly, I know Culsworth and he's a man of the highest reputation. Such a thing is quite impossible I assure you.'

'You would say that,' said Mr Baker. 'Dog don't eat dog.'

'I tell it to you,' said Panter, 'because it is as certain as anything can be in this uncertain world.'

'So you won't show him up for the blackguard he is?'

'Mr Baker,' said Panter, 'if I had evidence that a barrister, however eminent, had behaved disgracefully, I shouldn't hesitate to cross-examine him about it. The fact that Mr Culsworth is a QC of the highest repute would most certainly not deter me from putting to him that he was telling a lie, if there were reasonable evidence that he was. It is perfectly possible that he did not hear what you said, or did not take it in, or conceivably even that he forgot it. That can happen to anyone. But it is quite impossible that, knowing that you had said it, he deliberately said you hadn't.'

'That's what you say,' said Mr Baker. 'But it didn't happen to you. If you tell a bloke something and he says you didn't, you'd say he was lying wouldn't you?'

'Not necessarily at all. It depends on the circumstances. In Mr Culsworth's case he wanted to help you, not hurt you. There was no point in his lying about it, unless, as you suggest, he was bribed by the other side – and that's quite a ludicrous suggestion. He's been at the Bar many years and, if that's the sort of thing he did, he'd have been found out and disbarred ages ago, and probably sent to prison into the bargain.'

'Don't barristers never tell lies?'

'Certainly not in the course of their profession.'

'Not never?'

'Well, I can't answer for every barrister on every occasion. There must, of course, be a few black sheep, but Mr Culsworth most certainly isn't one of them.'

'Then you won't suggest he's telling lies?'

'Certainly not. And it wouldn't be in your interest for me to do so.'

'If I could prove it was a lie?'

'Obviously that would alter the position. If you could prove that he'd received money from the other side – and let me make it plain that such a thing is quite inconceivable – if you could prove that, or anything else as sinister, I shouldn't hesitate to cross-examine him on those lines. Or if he was a man who'd been up before his Benchers for proved misconduct in the course of a case, or something like that, I might be prepared to cross-examine him more roughly. But I can assure you that, as things stand, the only way to deal with him is to suggest that he made a mistake. It would be quite disastrous from your point of view to do anything else.'

'And it wouldn't be so hot for you either?' queried Mr Baker.

'No,' said Panter, 'you're perfectly right. I think I could very properly be criticised for suggesting that Mr Culsworth was deliberately – I repeat, deliberately – letting you down. The present evidence doesn't justify such an accusation.'

'And what d'you think will happen in the case?'

'It's impossible to say. It's your word against the defendant's.'

'But if the judge thinks I'm telling a lie about what I said to Mr Culsworth, that may be against me.'

'Yes, if he thinks you're telling a lie, it will.'

'Then it's a bit important, ain't it, that he shouldn't think I was telling a lie?'

'It's very important.'

'And if *he* was telling a lie, *I* wasn't.'

'I've already explained that, if he was mistaken, or might reasonably have been mistaken, that is quite sufficient from your point of view.'

'But if you could show that he was a crook, it would be better still?'

'Well, of course, but that's quite impossible. And let me make it plain that not only would you be very foolish to attempt to do such a thing but you would have to find another counsel to do it and, I expect, another solicitor. What d'you say, Mr Menton?'

Menton woke with a start.

'I'm so sorry,' he said, 'I didn't quite catch what you said.'

CHAPTER FIFTEEN

Mr Sampson's Activities

A few days after his call on Culsworth, Mr Sampson called on some chambers two blocks away from his. The head of the chambers was Andrew Lanoothin, a Welshman, whose ancestors had adopted an English spelling of their name. Mr Sampson asked to see the senior clerk.

'That's me,' said the clerk, Thomas Brinley. 'What can I do for you?'

'My name's Sampson.'

'How d'you do, Mr Sampson?'

'Well enough, thank you. And you?'

'Mustn't grumble.'

'Good,' said Mr Sampson. 'I like people who don't grumble. Lot of names you've got on the wall. Do any of them grumble?'

'Some of the younger ones do, if they don't get enough work,' said Thomas. 'Now, what can I do for you, Mr Sampson? Not from Sampson Musgrove, I suppose?'

'Musgrove?'

'No, Merivale. I'm always mixing up the names. It's Simmonds Musgrove. Sampson Merivale.'

'Most confusing. Nice view you have out of that window.'

'It is, isn't it? You want to brief someone in chambers?'

'Brief someone?'

'I thought you must be a solicitor.'

'I take it as a compliment. But I suppose there are all sorts.'

'They certainly vary. But what can I do for you? If it's insurance I'm afraid everyone's fixed up here.'

'Insurance? Extraordinary how everyone thinks I'm selling insurance. No, it's not insurance. I couldn't sell insurance. Do I look as though I could? Frankly, do I?'

'Well, what is it then, Mr Sampson?'

'I'll tell you an odd thing.'

Thomas waited.

'I've forgotten. I'm terribly sorry. I really have forgotten. I'll come back again another day when I've remembered. So very sorry to have troubled you. But don't forget.'

'Forget what?'

'You mustn't grumble.'

And without another word Mr Sampson left.

'What on earth?' said Thomas to himself aloud. 'Out of a looney-bin, I suppose. Oh, well,' and he took a ledger from a shelf and started to make some entries in it. Later that day he asked some of his colleagues if Mr Sampson had called on them. Culsworth's clerk said that he had.

'But he came to see the governor, not me. Very odd. He seemed to upset him.'

Meanwhile Mr Sampson was making his way round the Temple. Every now and then he stopped at a set of chambers, knocked, and had a similar kind of conversation with the clerk or the junior clerk as he had had with Andrew Lanoothin's clerk. Sometimes he said rather more. For example, when he called on the chambers on the ground floor of Alverstone Court, he mentioned his name and said he was a journalist.

'I'm afraid we've nothing for you here,' said the clerk. 'We can't talk about cases to the Press.'

'Well, I know you shouldn't,' said Mr Sampson.

'We don't,' said the clerk.

'Does a barrister a bit of good to get his name in the papers. D'you mean to say you never say a word off the record?'

The clerk hesitated for a moment.

'How rude of me,' said Mr Sampson. 'Please don't trouble to answer. But, as a matter of fact, it wasn't about any particular case I came. I'm really an enquiry agent but I do a bit of writing on the side. I want to do an article about the Bar generally, you know. Fees and all that. It's a closed book to most of the public.'

'Well, I haven't much time,' said the clerk, 'and I don't want to be quoted.'

'Of course not. Strictly off the record. Very good of you to talk to me at all. Fees, for example?'

'What about them?'

'Well, you can't sue for them. D'you always get paid?'

'Usually.'

'Ever do work on spec?'

'Not likely. It's unprofessional, anyway.'

'You mean your principal would get into trouble if you took a case on the terms no win, no fee?'

'It's I who'd get into trouble.'

'But if he knew about it?'

'Then it wouldn't happen. Anyway, I wouldn't do it.'

'Of course, there are ways and means. I mean to say, you could take a case for a very low fee and put it up if you won.'

'That's just as bad,' said the clerk.

'But is it never done?'

'Not here anyway. You'd have to alter the fee on the brief.'

'That's easy enough. A new back-sheet, for example.'

'What is all this?' asked the clerk. 'You seem to know a good deal. What are you after?'

'Nothing,' said Sampson, 'except information. Ever raised the fee when you saw the judge was in your favour?'

'I'm afraid I've given you all the time I can,' said the clerk.

'Sorry you're so touchy,' said Mr Sampson, 'but I'm sure you wouldn't have done any of those things – or any of the others I was going to ask you about if you'd had the chance.'

'Good morning. There's the door,' said the clerk.

'If I were a suspicious person,' said Mr Sampson, 'I should wonder why you've suddenly become so unfriendly. But fortunately I'm not at all suspicious. I never do a thing on suspicion. I want proof. Absolute proof. The documents, you know, or something like that.'

'Get out,' said the clerk.

'Of course,' said Mr Sampson. 'Silly of me not to bring the documents with me.'

'What documents?'

The clerk was unable to resist asking the question.

'Oh, never mind,' said Mr Sampson. 'They're of very doubtful authenticity. They'd never stand up in court. At least, I doubt if they would. Not at present, anyway. Good morning. So good of you to have co-operated.'

It was not long before Mr Sampson's activities were being discussed in the Temple, first among the clerks but very soon among the Bar. A blackmailer was in the Temple. Somehow or other he had obtained information of improper practices by barristers or their clerks and he was about to prey on them, if he could, unmercifully. The few barristers and clerks of the worst kind began to be really frightened, while even clerks in respectable chambers began to consider what peccadilloes they might have committed which could be made the subject matter of a complaint. Culsworth never told anyone of the definite threat to himself, but it soon became known that Sampson had in fact called on him. The slightly exaggerated statements of fact, which were exchanged between clerks at 'The Feathers' soon became wild rumours.

'Have you heard that he demanded £10,000 from X?'

'What for?'

'Well, you remember the sawdust case. X was for the plaintiff. I thought myself at the time that the way the case ended was pretty odd. Well, it seems that in fact he actually went to see the defendant himself and persuaded him to withdraw his defence.'

'Not really?'

'Well, that's what I heard. And on pretty good authority, too. Now the fellow's threatened to report him to his Benchers. As an alternative he suggested £10,000.'

'What's he going to do?'

'He's bound to go to the police. Once you pay these fellows, life's not worth living. Glad I've a clear conscience. Must be pretty awful to be blackmailed.'

'Has he gone to any solicitors, d'you know?'

'Not so far as I've heard. It's only the Temple. And Lincoln's Inn, I suppose, as well.'

Merely from these last words the rumour spread that a Chancery junior of the highest respectability, who had never been guilty of a questionable act or omission in the whole of his professional life, was being threatened with ruin. Barristers are no more immune from the ravages of rumour than any other portion of society. The stories spread through the Temple and Lincoln's Inn with alarming embellishment and rapidity.

Soon the judiciary became involved. And the most unlikely stories about them gained credence in certain quarters. No one suggested that a judge had actually taken a bribe in money, but there were several stories of good-looking female litigants unexpectedly winning their cases and being seen coming out of judges' flats in the early hours of the morning. It was soon 'discovered' that a divorce judge had pronounced a decree in favour of a near relation in a case reeking of collusion, and that another judge in the same division had pronounced in favour of a will which benefited an ex-mistress of his son-in-law when any other judge would have held that the signature was not the testator's, that it was not properly witnessed anyway, and that if it had been the testator's signature he was not of sound mind, memory or understanding when he signed it and that his signature (if any) was obtained by fraud or undue influence. To such an extent did rumour triumph that, for a very short time, it was actually suggested that a judge had sat on appeal from one of his own decisions and complimented 'the learned judge in the Court below' on the felicitous way in which he had given his judgment. This one did not last long, but another one did better. This alleged that Mr Justice Pigeon had tried a case in which he had appeared as counsel before he was made a judge and in which the client was his father-in-law.

Even the House of Lords did not escape. It was confidently asserted that two Law Lords had collided with one another in their cars while drunk, that they had been removed to the police station shouting legal tags at one another, that the police surgeon had at first certified that they were unfit by reason of alcohol, giving as one of his reasons that they were pretending to be Lords of Appeal, and that, on discovering that they were, he had destroyed his certificate. Finally, it was said, the police had sent them home in a police car after suggesting that a generous donation to the police benevolent funds might not be out of place.

Minor allegations which everyone really believed (though there was no foundation for any of them) were that at least half-a-dozen judges had found excuses for adjourning their courts in the middle of the day in order to go to Lords, Wimbledon or Ascot.

Metropolitan magistrates were soon drawn in. Apart from scurrilous suggestions that some of them had written protesting at the effect of the Street Offences Act, on the ground that it deprived their courts of colour, it was alleged that, in order to get through the lists quickly, defendants were invited to plead guilty to motoring offences by offers to reduce the fine – and were then fined double in order that this should not appear to have been the case. On the other hand, the pace was slowed down a bit by such obvious *canards* as the suggestion that a magistrate, who had an ulcer, had dismissed a charge of drunken driving brought against a distinguished surgeon, who had thereupon operated free of charge upon the magistrate and killed him.

Although there was little, if any, foundation for any of the rumours which spread, Mr Sampson's activities were taken very seriously in the Temple. Barristers and clerks began to search their consciences. Benchers of the Inns began to wonder if the latitude allowed to practitioners at the Criminal Bar in the conduct of their cases was not becoming abused. Did the Bar need pulling together?

The Temple is not far from Fleet Street and it was not long before paragraphs started to appear in the newspapers. They were, of course, in general terms. No editor was going to take the risk of a libel action by a barrister or his clerk, let alone a judge. But you cannot libel a whole profession, and journalists, particularly those who disliked the law or lawyers, started to raise queries about the standard of integrity at the Bar.

'It is said,' ran one article, 'that a blackmailer is going the rounds of the Temple and Lincoln's Inn threatening to report barristers and their clerks for unprofessional behaviour, but offering to refrain – on terms. Now, there are few crimes worse than blackmail, but, while one can have sympathy for the victim and disgust for the criminal, it is seldom possible to blackmail anyone unless he has done something wrong. The fact that so many people in the law appear to be vulnerable to this despicable mode of attack suggests that the high-sounding phrases about barristers' integrity, which are so regularly and sanctimoniously used both by the Bar itself and the Bench, need perhaps to be reconsidered. If one man can reduce one side of the legal profession to a state of shivering anxiety, is it not time that that side of the profession asks itself if all is well within it? Is it not time that it took steps to clean up its stables so that there should be no material for the blackmailer to use and in consequence no victims upon whom he can prey? Undoubtedly this man, whoever he is, should be caught quickly and sent to prison for many years but, when that has been done, the Bar should not just lick its wounds but should consider what surgical operations may be necessary to see that such a state of affairs cannot occur again.'

CHAPTER SIXTEEN

More of Mr Sampson

Meanwhile Mr Sampson, either oblivious of the stir which he was causing or quite unconcerned by it, continued his activities. On one occasion a clerk looking out of a window saw him first examine the names at the entrance to the staircase, make a few notes, and then lean up against the wall and light a cigarette. The clerk, who was a most respectable clerk in a most respectable set of chambers, spoke to one of his employers, Stephen Ferndown, a moderately able member of the Bar who was of the gruff, forthright type who didn't believe in wrapping things up. He called fraud fraud and not misrepresentation and, while reasonably polite to the Bench, he used a minimum of the phrases 'with great respect,' 'if I may respectfully say so,' 'when your Lordship was good enough to indicate,' 'I'm most obliged to your Lordship,' 'if I might venture to disagree with your Lordship,' 'I'm loth to interrupt my learned friend,' 'my learned friend is always the soul of courtesy,' etc. etc. Instead he would say such things as: 'Your Lordship is entirely wrong,' 'your Lordship has misunderstood the evidence,' 'if your Lordship would look at the evidence as a whole instead of picking on one or two sentences out of their context,' 'will my learned friend kindly keep quiet while I am speaking,' and so forth.

Mr Ferndown decided to have it out with Mr Sampson. He folded up the papers which he had been reading, and went straight downstairs.

'Good morning,' said Mr Sampson.'

'Are you looking for someone?' asked Ferndown.

'Yes and no,' said Mr Sampson.

'What d'you mean by that?'

'What d'you think I mean?'

'I've no idea.'

'So you still want to know.'

'That's why I asked you.'

'That doesn't follow.'

'I repeat, it's why I asked you.'

'I repeat, it doesn't follow. Shall I tell you why it doesn't follow?'

'No.'

'Then we're back where we started. Shall I begin again? Good morning.' Then, after a pause, he added: 'Sir.'

'What are you doing here?' demanded Ferndown.

'The same as the rest of us.'

'What d'you mean by that?'

'What d'you think I mean?'

Ferndown tried again.

'The Temple is private property. Have you any legitimate business here?'

'Have I?'

'Yes, have you?'

'You tell me.'

'I shall do no such thing.'

'All right. You're excused. You may fall out.'

'If you have no legitimate business here I shall arrange with the authorities to have you ejected.'

'Off you go and arrange,' said Mr Sampson. 'Where shall I be when you come back?'

'I warn you that loitering is not permitted.'

'What's loitering, may I ask? As a matter of fact I have a few calls to pay and in the meantime I'm wandering around enjoying the peace here – until you interrupted, rather brusquely if I may say so. And if I may proceed from there,' continued Mr Sampson, 'may I know what right you have to question me in this way as though you yourself were the owner of this place and I were a tramp trespassing upon your property? I am doing no more than hundreds or thousands of Londoners do every day. What right have you to question my activities?'

'My clerk saw you making notes outside these chambers.'

'I dare say he saw you making notes inside them. If you'll show me yours, I might show you mine. I don't promise, mind you, but I might. Might I know your name, sir?'

'Certainly not.'

'You are beginning to annoy me, sir,' said Mr Sampson. 'You come up to me quite unprovoked and begin to cross-examine me as though I were a witness in one of your beastly boxes. Might I suggest, sir, that you reserve your cross-examination for the places where you have a right to conduct it? Might I also point out that I have a hasty temper, sir, and that your unmannerly behaviour is making my fingers itch? Perhaps you could inform me whether conduct likely to provoke a breach of the peace is an offence within the confines of the Temple, or whether one has to go out into the Strand to commit it? Because, if it can be committed here, you are close on committing it, sir. Kindly go back to your lair, sir, or whatever you call the place from which you sprang upon me. I do not propose to continue this conversation. I shall make as many notes as I please and I shall call upon as many people as I please and lean against as many walls as I please and I shall not ask your permission, sir, neither by word of mouth, nor by writing nor by conduct. I end as I began, good morning.'

And Mr Sampson leaned against the wall and took a puff at his cigarette. Ferndown, without another word, went upstairs and reported the facts to the office of the Under-Treasurer. Meanwhile Mr Sampson paid a call on Margaret.

'I hoped you'd be in,' he said. 'In fact I waited till you were.'

'I tell you there's nothing I can give you,' said Margaret. 'Why don't you go for somebody who's worth something? I'm not.'

'Who d'you suggest?'

'I've no idea.'

'Oh – come, now. You made the suggestion. I'm not unreasonable. I'm always open to a good offer. If you could put me on to something good, I might forget all about the Fisherman's Nook – for a time, anyway. Until you win a football pool or something. Come on now. Give me a lead.'

'There's nothing I can tell you.'

'Surely you know something bad about someone – other than yourself? What about those barristers down below? You know them, I suppose?'

'Some of them. Not terribly well. I know nothing against them.'

'They're a rum lot, I must say. Went to see one of them. Fellow called Culsworth. Know him?'

'A little.'

'Now there's something wrong there, I can tell you. Must be.'

'I'm sure there isn't.'

'But you only know him a little. How can you be sure? He might have done something for all you know. Anything for which he hasn't been found out, I mean. And I can tell you there is something.'

'Well, why don't you ...'

'Why don't I turn my attentions to him? Because I don't know what it is – yet.'

'How do you know there is anything?'

'Because he let me see him. He didn't know my name, he didn't know my business, he knew I wasn't a solicitor, and yet without a word, without a question, he saw me. Now why, I ask you. A man in his position isn't going to see any chap that calls on him without an introduction and without knowing his business first. What's your explanation?'

'Explanation? I haven't any. It is strange.'

'Unless, of course,' went on Mr Sampson, 'You've consulted him about our little affair. Why didn't I think of that before? Is that what you've done? Don't bother to answer. But it would account for his seeing me, wouldn't it? What a pity. I felt sure it was something else. Oh well, it means we'll have to concentrate on the Fisherman's Nook. I'm sorry. But business is business. And I can't afford to waste my time. Spending is one thing. Wasting is another. I'm afraid I shall have to have some results very soon now. Why not sell that piece over there? Must be worth quite a bit.'

'My husband would miss it.'

'Tell him you've had an accident and it's gone for repair.'

'He'd want to know where, and to see the estimate.'

'Oh, a mean man, is he? You'll be well rid of him. I shall have to tell him, you know. For the sake of example, if nothing else. Suppose you simply can't make me an offer, suppose I really believed you couldn't – I don't, but just suppose – then if I just went off and left things as they were, everyone else would play the same game and I'd get nowhere. So, if you really can't help me, I shall have to tell your husband. Self-preservation you can call it, if you like. But whatever you call it, it's a fact, as you'll discover. D'you believe me?'

'I'm afraid I do,' said Margaret.

'Good,' said Mr Sampson. 'You've no idea what a lot of trouble and anxiety it would save if everyone believed me. No, don't see me out. I'm getting to know my way quite well. But I shan't come much more. Don't forget, I spend time, not waste it. Believe me.'

CHAPTER SEVENTEEN

Scotland Yard Intervenes

As soon as Mr Sampson had left, Margaret telephoned to
know if she might see Culsworth and he arranged to see
her the same day. As soon as they met she told him what
had happened and it worried him more than he showed.

'I'm afraid what's happening is that he's going to make
an example of you so as to encourage any other people in
the Temple to pay up.'

'D'you know any of them?' asked Margaret.

'I've heard some of the rumours,' said Culsworth
uncomfortably, 'but most of them are pretty wild, though
he certainly knows something. If only someone would
prosecute. But they're frightened to.'

'You'd like me to prosecute, wouldn't you?' said
Margaret.

'Quite frankly I would,' said Culsworth, 'but I do see
your point of view. Of course, everything would be done
to help you keep the knowledge from your husband.'

'How sure are you that it could be kept from him?' It
was a difficult question for him to answer. It was quite
clear now that Sampson would stop at nothing and that,
if he were not paid, he would reveal the information, even
though it meant that he got nothing out of that
transaction. He had said so to Margaret. He would be

looking to the other transactions to make up. That meant that sooner or later disclosure would come for him. Perhaps even in the Baker case, which would soon be coming on for trial. But if Sampson were prosecuted first, there would be a chance of disclosure being avoided or at least postponed. If Sampson went to prison he might prefer to retain the information undisclosed for use when he came out. Well, he might get fourteen or even forty-two years and might die in prison. So, from his point of view, a prosecution by Margaret at once would provide a real hope of safety. But the chance of her husband not learning of it could not fairly be said to be large. It was a possibility, but nothing more.

He thought for some time before answering.

'Mrs Verney,' he said eventually, 'I should very much like you to. prosecute. In saying that, I must admit that I am thinking more of other people than of you. On the other hand, if you do nothing and can't pay him, he'll tell your husband, as he said he would. So, if you can't keep him at bay any longer, it seems to me that you have less to lose by prosecuting than by doing nothing. To do nothing means that your husband will be told for a certainty, to prosecute at least gives you a chance that he'll never know. I do hope,' he added, 'that I'm not being too much influenced by my anxiety for other people's sake that you should prosecute.'

'Thank you for being so fair,' said Margaret, 'but you speak so seriously that I could almost believe that you were personally involved yourself.'

He hesitated for a moment. Then: 'I am, Mrs Verney,' he said.

It was not as good as telling his Benchers, but it was something. And his conscience gave him an encouraging pat.

'All right,' she said, 'I'll agree. What do we do?'

'You should go straight to the police and tell them what's happened. I'll go with you, if you like.'

'That's very good of you. When and where shall we go?'

'We'll go to Scotland Yard. And as soon as possible.'

There was indeed necessity for hurry from Culsworth's point of view. The retrial of the Baker case was due very shortly. It was very important, he considered, to let Sampson know the game was up before that case started.

Next day they went to Scotland Yard together. On the way Culsworth mentioned that he was not going to say anything about his own troubles.

'I quite understand,' Margaret said. 'As far as I am concerned you can forget that you said anything to me, but I appreciated it more than I can say.'

At Scotland Yard they were interviewed by a Detective Superintendent. Like everyone else he had heard the rumours and he was naturally glad that he was going to get something concrete to enable him to catch the man.

'When d'you expect a further call from him?' Margaret was asked.

'I can never tell. But very soon.'

'Well, I think,' said the superintendent, 'that I'll have to plant a couple of men in your flat for a few days.'

'D'you mean to stay?'

'If you don't mind.'

'Of course I don't mind, but what'll my husband say?'

'Oh, of course, I forgot,' said the superintendent. 'But, you see, the trouble is that this sort of chap is pretty fly and probably knows all about traps. If he sees two men walk up your staircase he may easily guess they're police officers. And that'll be that. Could we perhaps use your chambers, sir?'

'I don't see why not,' said Culsworth. 'But how are they going to eat and sleep?'

'Well, I don't see why they should sleep there, sir. The man doesn't come when Mrs Verney's husband's around. So, if they can come pretty early in the morning and leave at night, that should be all right. As for food, I expect they can manage. No doubt you've a gas ring or something they can use?'

'Or I can bring something down for them,' suggested Margaret.

'That's very good of you, madam. I'm sure they'd appreciate it. Have to be a bit careful how it's done, though. In case he's watching the place. Well, I'll send Inspector Drewe and a sergeant to wire the place up as soon as your husband has left. What time would that be?'

'You'd better make it 9.30. He's always gone by then.'

'Very well then. Of course I don't know how long I can keep two officers on the job. But it's a very serious case and, in view of the other people affected, I think it'll be justified.'

So the inspector and the sergeant came to the Temple, fixed microphones in the sitting room of the Verneys' flat and connected them up to a room in Culsworth's chambers which was made available for the purpose. Three days went by and Mr Sampson did not appear, but on the fourth day, when the police were considering replacing the two officers by a recording machine, he arrived. It had been arranged that each time before she opened the door to a caller Margaret was to alert the police officers by pressing a bell. Then, if the caller were not Mr Sampson, she should tell them so.

As soon as she had let him in, she took him into the sitting room and the police officers below remained on the alert.

'I'm sorry to have left you alone for so long,' said Mr Sampson, after he had taken a chair, 'but I've been awfully busy. A terrible lot of people to see. I hope you'll forgive me.'

'Of course.'

'Now, what were we discussing last time I called? To tell you the truth I've been doing so much since I last saw you that I've almost forgotten what I've been coming to see you about.'

'I haven't,' said Margaret.

'That's natural. You've only the one case – I've hundreds. Or they seem like that. Same with a judge, I suppose. The prisoner remembers the judge all right, but the judge can't be expected to remember the prisoner. He sees too many of them.'

'I suppose so.'

'Well, what point had we reached?'

'You mentioned how good the view was from one of the rooms in the Fisherman's Nook Hotel.'

'I may well have done. As a matter of fact most of the rooms there have a good view. It's a very nice little place. Ever stayed there?'

Margaret did not answer.

'You'll have to book well in advance if you want to go in the season, you know. It gets very full up. Incidentally, you've got rather a nice view from here yourself.'

'You said that the first time you came.'

'At least it shows I'm consistent. Now what did I come to see you for?'

He looked round the room and then got up.

'Do forgive me,' he said, as he moved a chair. 'I'm interested in so many things. Furniture. And pictures. That's charming.'

He pointed to a picture on the wall and lifted it up. Then he shook his head. He looked under a desk and then kneeled down and raised a corner of the carpet, without saying anything. He got up and shook his head again.

'My memory,' he said. 'It's terrible. D'you know, I haven't the faintest idea what I came for. And now I've wasted your time and mine. I'm so very sorry.'

And, without giving Margaret any time to say anything, he left the room and the flat abruptly.

After making sure that he had left the building the police officers and Culsworth went up to see Margaret. Culsworth was now desperately worried.

'He obviously realised there was a trap,' said Inspector Drewe. 'So he's not likely to fall for another.'

'I'm afraid that's so,' said Culsworth. 'You could, I suppose, arrest him on the information given by Mrs Verney, or obtain a warrant for his arrest on that information, but if he denies everything, as no doubt he will, there won't be much prospect of getting a conviction on Mrs Verney's uncorroborated evidence.'

'What about one of the other people in the Temple?' suggested the inspector. 'D'you think any of them would talk?'

'You could try,' said Culsworth, and kept his eyes off Margaret.

'I doubt if we'll get anything,' said the inspector. 'People who are being blackmailed are pretty shy of talking. That's what makes our job so difficult in these cases.'

'I see that,' said Culsworth.

'We could point out that it's a public duty to get this chap,' said the inspector. 'That might have some effect, don't you think? After all, we're dealing with lawyers, who understand that sort of thing, not just with irresponsible people who think only of their own skins.'

103

'I'm afraid,' said Culsworth, 'that, when publicity may mean ruin, lawyers will not be found to be very different from other people. Indeed, it's worse for anyone in the Temple. Anyone outside the law has some chance of remaining anonymous, but a lawyer has none. And that will apply equally to barristers' clerks. However, you might have a try.'

'Well, we'll do that, sir,' said the inspector. 'What are we going to do if we get nothing?'

'That's up to you, of course,' said Culsworth, 'but I suppose you could interview Sampson and put Mrs Verney's story to him? You might get some corroboration of it in that way, either by some admission that he makes or by some obviously false story which he puts up on the spur of the moment.'

'I doubt if there's going to be any "spur of the moment" with this customer,' said the inspector. 'If he hasn't his story cut and dried I shall be very surprised. However, I think you're right, sir. That'll be the best thing to do if we can get no information of value from anyone else.'

So Inspector Drewe and the sergeant started making enquiries in the Temple. They acquired a certain amount of information about Mr Sampson's visits but nothing which could remotely be made the subject matter of a charge. Moreover it appeared to the inspector that, in some cases at any rate, the people whom they interviewed hardly liked even to admit that Mr Sampson had called on them at all. Their reluctance suggested that, if Mr Sampson thought that they were worth a visit, people might think there was something in their professional lives which they did not want to disclose.

After a week of careful enquiries the police found nothing to add to Mrs Verney's statement and so they decided to tax Mr Sampson with her allegations against him. Just at this time Mr Baker's case came on for trial. And Culsworth's hopes of a prosecution before then were ended.

CHAPTER EIGHTEEN

Mr Baker's Case Retried

The judge was Mr Justice Reddish and he sat with a jury. After the jury had been sworn, Panter opened the case for Mr Baker.

'Members of the jury,' he began, 'once a week for a majority of the weeks in the year a large number of people in this country including, I expect, some of you, have a genuine hope that the whole of their lives may be changed. That, instead of sharing the kitchen and bathroom with their next door neighbours or their mothers-in-law, they will have a house of their own. That, instead of wondering whether they can find the next instalment due on the car, they will own a car outright. That husbands will be able to give fur coats to their wives. That wives will be able quite easily to get all the clothes which the children need. That they won't have to scrape and save for a week's holiday in a third rate boarding house but will be able to take a trip round the world. For most people there is no other hope of this kind available. They have no elderly relations likely to die and leave them a lot of money. They have no large endowment policies about to mature. The only hope they have is that they may have sent in a winning line in a football pool. No one pretends that this is more than a slender hope, but it is a real one. Nearly every week one person at least receives a big prize. P'raps it'll be me next time, they say. The fact that they are much more likely, as far as statistics are concerned, to be run over in the street doesn't lessen the hope.'

The judge, who had started to grow impatient after the first few sentences, could restrain himself no longer.

'What on earth has all this got to do with the case, Mr Panter?'

'If your Lordship will allow me to continue my address to the jury, your Lordship will be enlightened on the matter,' said Panter, quite unruffled.

'I've read the pleadings,' said the judge, 'and all this flummery appears to me to be wholly irrelevant.'

'The jury,' said Mr Panter, 'have not had your Lordship's advantage of reading the pleadings.'

'Then why don't you tell the jury what is in the pleadings, instead of pouring out this frothy nonsense?'

'I'm sorry, my Lord,' said Panter, 'but, subject to any directions by your Lordship, I propose to open the case to the jury in my own way and to come to the pleadings when it seems convenient. There are, as far as I know, no particular rules as to how counsel should or should not open a case.'

'There is certainly one rule – that what he says should be relevant,' said the judge. 'If the plaintiff is entitled to share in the defendant's prize, it doesn't matter in the least what are the hopes or thoughts of other people who go in for these competitions. If you want to write an article on the modern desire for obtaining something for nothing, no doubt you could send it to the *Economist* or *The Times*, but I would suggest, even in that case, that you leave out some of the trimmings.'

'At the moment,' said Panter, 'I am hoping to be allowed to address the jury in this case on behalf of the plaintiff and not to pursue the journalistic activities your Lordship is good enough to suggest.'

'Well, suppose you tell the jury what the case is about?' said the judge.

'With your Lordship's permission,' said Panter, 'I will continue to do so.'

It may be wondered why an advocate of Panter's obvious ability should appear almost deliberately to get on bad terms with the judge before the case had been going five minutes. There was a reason. On the whole judges try to control their personal likes and dislikes. Those who hate motor cycles, try hard to decide fairly any accident case which involves such a vehicle. Judges who are allergic to noise do not automatically grant injunctions to restrain defendants from carrying out some noisy operation, which the judge himself could not bear to have next door. But they are only human and, for example, a judge who is devoted to animals might, at any rate unconsciously, decide a case where cruelty to animals is involved rather differently from a judge who was not interested in them. Mr Justice Reddish loathed any form of gambling. He considered it a sign of degeneration that so much of the time of the country was occupied in this way. And, as he watched the tendency grow, as he found betting shops licensed, football pools vastly increasing, and even the Government inviting the public to gamble, he became more and more obsessed with the subject. When he was a young man the prizes for the most part went to those who had worked for them, who had given brain or brawn or both in pursuit of them. There was, of course, some gambling but it didn't compare with what goes on today. The downfall of the Roman Empire was partly due, he believed, to the loss of moral fibre in the population. Gambling saps the moral fibre of those who indulge in it. Something for nothing, is their cry. Instead of hard work, the throw of dice was to decide what reward a man was to have. He had expressed these opinions more than once in strong language. Panter accordingly felt that the judge would not care in the least whether Mr Baker shared the defendant's winnings or not. Indeed, he might well feel that it served the plaintiff right for having gone in for the competition and that it would teach him, and perhaps others, a salutary lesson if, even though the dice turned up in his favour, he nevertheless got nothing. Panter, therefore, decided that the judge would be against him throughout the action and, rightly or wrongly, he thought it would be good tactics on his part to bait the judge at the very beginning and in that way to try to enlist the sympathy of the jury and make them less likely to be influenced by the judge's remarks.

So Panter continued to address the jury while the judge did little to conceal his impatience, now looking pathetically at the jury and now sighing and looking up to the ceiling.

While this performance was going on in Queen's Bench Court 1, a more dramatic performance was going on in Court 2 – though only one person, Culsworth, was aware of the drama. He was conducting a case before Mr Justice Pellet, but, although he was trying hard to concentrate on his work, he found it impossible not to think from time to time of the case going on next door, and wonder when he would be required to go there. He had informed the judge of the possibility of his being required to give evidence but no one could have told from the almost nonchalant manner in which he referred to the matter how much it meant to him. He tried to suppress the sickening flutter in his stomach, which everyone has experienced from time to time, from the days when a visit had to be paid to the headmaster to the days of war.

Culsworth found it difficult indeed to concentrate on the Building (Safety, Health and Welfare) Regulations 1948, and to deal with questions of fact which gave rise to a consideration of these regulations. How could he really devote his mind to the question why a building collapsed when in his view his whole life might be collapsing within a few hours?

Next door Panter at last completed his opening and called Mr Baker into the witness box. He explained how it had come about that the defendant and he had agreed to go in for the pools together that week, and what his suggestions had been for filling in the coupon.

'Have I got to learn how these beastly things work?' asked the judge. 'Will that be necessary for the purposes of the case?'

'It's simple, me Lord,' said Mr Baker, 'if you keep off the perms.'

'Keep off the perms?' repeated the judge distastefully. 'What on earth does that mean?'

'Permutations, my Lord,' said Panter. 'But your Lordship won't have to bother about them for the purposes of this case.'

'Well, that's something,' said the judge. 'I suppose it's too much to hope that the majority of the jury know as little as I do about these things.'

This *was* too much for one of the jurymen. He got up.

'Forgive me, my Lord,' he said, 'but I'm very fond of the pools. I go in each week and I enjoy it. I don't expect to win, but there's always the chance and I enjoy filling in the coupon.'

'Sit down and behave yourself,' said the judge.

Another member of the jury rose and smiled ingratiatingly.

'I think the poolth are a dithgrathe,' he lisped.

'You sit down too,' said the judge. The case was getting a little out of hand. Members of the public would be speaking from the gallery or the body of the court if he weren't careful.

Mr Baker continued his evidence and this time Panter saw to it that he brought the interview at the public house more into the forefront. Then he was cross-examined by Mr Hopkins.

'I suggest to you,' began Hopkins, 'that this action is just an attempt to get half of my client's winnings.'

'Well, of course it is,' said Mr Baker. 'I'm entitled to them.'

'I mean that you've trumped up the main part of your story.'

'What am I supposed to say to that?'

'Is your story true, or have you invented it?' asked the judge.

'I took an oath to tell the truth,' said Mr Baker.

'So do a lot of people,' said the judge. 'I expect Mr Potter is going to take the oath in this case.'

'He certainly is,' said Hopkins.

'Please don't interrupt when I'm speaking,' said the judge. 'I was saying that a lot of people take the oath. And often both sides take it. Both can't be right, and often one side must be telling lies. So the mere fact that you've taken the oath proves nothing.'

'Then what's the point of my taking it?' enquired Mr Baker.

'I sometimes wonder myself,' said the judge. 'But it's the law.'

'Well, if no one don't take no notice of it, it seems a pretty stupid law,' said Mr Baker.

'Now behave yourself, Mr Baker,' said the judge. 'You're here to answer questions, not to criticise legal procedure. Now, answer the question, please.'

'I've forgotten it, my Lord.'

'What was it, Mr Hopkins?'

'It was your Lordship's question.'

'I dare say it was, but what was it?'

'I'm afraid I've forgotten it. Perhaps the shorthand writer can help.'

'Very sorry, my Lord, but my pencil broke just at that moment.'

'You ought to have more than one.'

'I have, my Lord. I was reaching for the other.'

'Well, why didn't you say something?'

'I didn't like to interrupt.'

'Well, another time you must. You're supposed to get a complete and accurate note of all the evidence. I know it's impossible, and that no one ever does, but you've got to try.'

'I'm sorry, my Lord.'

'You'd better go on, Mr Hopkins,' said the judge.

'What I suggest you've done, Mr Baker, is this,' said Hopkins. 'You had two interviews with my client, I agree, but you've just twisted what was said at those interviews to suit your case.'

'I've twisted nothing. What did I give him ten and six for, if it wasn't half the stake?'

'I suggest you didn't give him anything.'

'Not give him anything? You ask him if a half-crown didn't fall on the ground and roll into some sawdust.'

'You've never said that before.'

'Well, I'm saying it now. I gave him four half-crowns and a tanner, and he dropped one of the half-crowns. And a black kitten ran after it and I said "That's a bit of luck." '

'You didn't say any of this at your first trial.'

'I'd forgotten it. But you ask him. He knows all right. He used to play with that kitten. Two-pint Kate he used to call her. He knows. And she was first on the half dollar!'

Hopkins spoke to Potter.

'I suggest to you that you've done the same with this piece of evidence as you've done with the rest. You're quite right. My client did drop half-a-crown and the kitten did run after it, but it was nothing to do with you. It was my client's own money.'

'Well, so it was,' said Mr Baker. 'I'd just given it to him to put on the pools, hadn't I? That means it was his money, don't it?'

'I suggest you hadn't given it to him at all.'

'Well, I had, see. And he spat on it for luck and all.'

Again Hopkins spoke to his client.

'That's quite right,' he went on. 'After he'd dropped it and the kitten had played with it, my client said it was his pools money and he spat on it for luck.'

'What was he getting out his pools money in the boozer for?' asked Mr Baker. 'He couldn't buy no postal orders there. He spat on it because I gave it to him.'

'Don't ask me questions,' said Hopkins.

'I wasn't,' said Mr Baker. 'I was telling you something, and he knows it's true. That's why you don't like it.'

'Be quiet,' said the judge. 'Don't make statements. Just answer the questions.'

'He doesn't ask me any,' complained Mr Baker. 'He just tells me I'm a liar.'

'What is the next question, Mr Hopkins?' said the judge.

'You say that since the writ my client in effect admitted his liability but said you couldn't prove it. I suggest to you that what really happened was that my client asked you what good you thought you could do by litigation when you knew you couldn't win.'

'Yes, he did say something like that,' said Mr Baker.

'And that's all he said?'

Mr Baker remained silent.

'Well?' said Hopkins.

'Well what?'

'D'you agree that that is all he said?'

'Of course not. I've told you. He said that no one saw me pay my share and that he could change his mind about sharing if he liked.'

'Now, on the first trial you swore that you told this to your counsel?'

'I did.'

'Do you know that he denies that any such thing happened?'

'Yes.'

'Why d'you think Mr Culsworth denied it?'

'Well, I think it's because he's a perishing liar, but my counsel says I mustn't say that and that it was all a mistake.'

'D'you know that we have subpoenaed him to give evidence?'

'Are you going to claim privilege, Mr Panter?' asked the judge.

'No, my Lord.'

'Very well, then,' said the judge, 'you may continue this line of cross-examination.'

'Well, Mr Baker,' said Hopkins, 'why should you think Mr Culsworth should tell lies to hurt your case? What reason could he have?'

'You ask *him* that,' said Mr Baker.

CHAPTER NINETEEN

Mrs Culsworth Tries Again

While Mr Baker was being cross-examined, the police were looking for Mr Sampson. No one knew his address but many people had seen him in the Temple and were very willing to assist the police. But he simply did not appear in the places which he had been frequenting for weeks.

Mr Baker's case started on a Friday and was adjourned the same day while he was still being cross-examined. Accordingly Culsworth still did not know when he would be called to give evidence, still less what he would be asked. The fact that the police had been unable to pick up Mr Sampson straight away neither relieved nor alarmed him. Counsel for Mr Potter must already have been instructed and either he had been told about the Moriarty case or he had not. Mr Sampson's disappearance – if the failure to find him for two or three days amounted to that – would not affect the matter.

During the weekend, Jane Culsworth made a last attempt to persuade her husband to deny the Moriarty charge if it were made.

'All these people are criminals,' she said. 'Moriarty himself, Mr Sampson and anyone else who gave him the information. Why should you ruin yourself because of them? Why give them the satisfaction?'

'I don't know whether it will or won't give them satisfaction, and I don't really care. I only know that I simply cannot stand up in the witness box and lie. Could you do it?'

'If your happiness were involved,' said Jane, 'most certainly I could and would. You may be right, and perhaps wives have a different sense of values from husbands. I only know that I should think it right to lie to save you. Incidentally, if I were charged with capital murder, would you give me away rather than tell an untruth?'

'The situation couldn't arise,' said Culsworth. 'If you'd been the kind of woman who could be guilty of capital murder, we'd never have been married.'

'Suppose I went off my head?'

'Then it wouldn't be murder. But this sort of argument just won't do. You can always put up an absurd example to try to prove a point.'

'Well, if I were charged with a serious motoring offence, would you lie to save me? Now that's not an impossible situation. Suppose I got drunk and did a lot of damage with the car and you could save me from prosecution and probable imprisonment by telling a lie, would you do it?'

'On oath?' asked Culsworth.

'There goes the lawyer,' said Jane. 'You want to know whether it would be on oath or not. No normal woman would want to know that. She'd lie without question to the police, to the magistrate, to the judge, to everyone to help her husband. I certainly would, and so would most women who adored their husbands. But I'll answer your question like the good lawyer's wife I am. First of all, would you lie to the police to save me? Secondly, would you lie in the witness box?'

Culsworth did not answer at once.

'To save me,' she repeated.

'I just don't know,' he answered eventually. 'We lawyers have been brought up to regard the truth as sacrosanct as far as we are concerned. I don't mean that lies by people outside the profession shock us. Of course not. We'd be out of business if there weren't lots of them. But a barrister's or solicitor's word we look upon as absolutely trustworthy – except, of course, in a very few cases of people who oughtn't to be in either profession.'

'But you don't mean that you expect every barrister or solicitor – or judge for that matter – who has a jealous wife and has kissed another woman, always to tell his wife the truth about it?'

'That's a purely personal matter, but even there I should be a bit shocked if I heard, say, Mr Justice Blank tell a lie to his wife. But I'm not really talking of such personal matters. I mean professionally it's automatic for us to tell the truth and it's almost impossible for us to do otherwise.'

'But if I were charged with something, you would only be acting as my husband, not as a lawyer. There'd be nothing professional about it.'

'That's true, but it would be a lie in connection with a case and every instinct in me would make me revolt at the thought of it.'

'What about having an instinct to preserve and help me? The other's stronger, is it? I'm not trying to rub it in, but I must say I find it a little hard that you were prepared to lie professionally for a thug like Moriarty and that you wouldn't lie privately for me.'

'That's perfectly fair,' said Culsworth. 'I acted disgracefully. It would be nothing like as disgraceful to lie to protect you. But now I'm probably in a worse position than other lawyers. Because of my behaviour in Moriarty's case, I am more determined than ever that I shan't offend again. And, in this particular case, don't forget I should be lying to save myself in the first place, and you only secondarily. If you'd been involved in a car accident I should be lying primarily to save you and secondly for myself.'

'Would you do it then?' she persisted.

'I just don't know,' he said. 'Thank the Lord the problem will never arise.'

'The problem has arisen.'

'What!' he said.

'No, I haven't been doing anything. I simply mean that all this legal talk of primarily and secondarily is nonsense. If you ruin yourself you ruin us at one and the same moment. You ruin us financially, physically, mentally, in every way. How will it be for me and the girls with my husband and their father disbarred? What about their careers? They're quite bright but not all that above average. There must be plenty as good. Who will the places at a university go to – to those with a disbarred father, or to two other girls whose father's a respectable bank clerk? And then, from the purely financial point of view, you've brought us up to enjoy a certain standard of living. That'll drop like a stone.'

'Not necessarily. I might get a good job in commerce as a legal adviser.'

'What! A disbarred barrister – who was disbarred for telling a lie!'

'Perhaps you're right. It'll be damned unfair to you and I don't suppose I can ever make it up to you. I deserve everything you say. It's simply that I know that I can't do it.'

'I'm sorry, darling,' she said more gently. 'I haven't meant to be hard. I was just fighting to try to convince you. But, as I haven't, we're in it together, as I said before. Whatever happens, there'll be no change between us.'

CHAPTER TWENTY

The Search for Mr Sampson

Mr Sampson not having appeared during the weekend, the police sought the help of the Press.

'The police would like to interview a Mr Sampson who, it is thought, may be able to help them in their enquiries into certain allegations. Mr Sampson was last seen in the area of the Temple, EC4 and, when calling on strangers, has a habit of admiring the view from their windows.'

Immediately a hue and cry was raised by the Press for Mr Sampson. The international situation was comparatively quiet and there had been no sensational bank robberies or murders. BLACKMAILER SOUGHT, their headlines proclaimed, and once again referred to some of the more lurid stories about Mr Sampson. Even the more cautious newspapers not only printed the police request but added a paragraph about his recent activities.

Then clues started to come in. Mr Sampson was in York. He was still in London. He was travelling up and down the country in a fast car. He had had a drink at the bar of a well-known hotel in. Manchester. He was making for the Continent. He had tried to hire a private aeroplane and lost his nerve at the last moment. The airports and seaports were being watched. And so on and so on.

But not one word was said about Mr or Mrs Verney although the Press knew all about them and that the prosecution, when it took place, would, in the first instance anyway, be based on her complaint. Allegations are often made against the British Press and are sometimes justified, but on occasions such as this they are capable of restraint which is probably not equalled in any place in the world. Like everyone else they loathe blackmail, and they were not going to do anything themselves to ruin Margaret's hopes of matrimonial happiness.

By the following weekend Mr Sampson had not appeared and the Sunday newspapers added to the publicity. There was not a national newspaper which did not join in the chase, and most of the provincial papers followed suit. A nationwide search was on and the hate engendered against Mr Sampson was very considerable. If he had suddenly been caught in a crowded area he would certainly have required police protection.

While the search was on, Mr Sampson himself walked into a quiet country hotel and asked for a room for a few days. He registered in the name of Sampson and, as he did so, he said with a smile: 'I'd better not mention the view, or you'd be ringing up the police.'

The receptionist looked at his entry, and smiled too.

'It must be rather embarrassing for you at the moment,' she said.

'I suppose it could be,' Mr Sampson replied, 'but it hasn't been so far.'

'Well, I can't see a man who's wanted up and down the country registering in his own name, if it's as uncommon as his.'

'Oh, I don't know,' said Mr Sampson. 'That'd be the most sensible thing to do. Perhaps you'd like me to give you a full account of my movements?'

'Of course not – except your future movements. How long will you be staying?'

'About a week, I should think. Perhaps a little longer, if that'll be all right.'

'Oh, certainly. We don't get full up at this time of year.'

The next day Mr Sampson went into the nearest town and entered the offices of Messrs Seaworthy, Clipper and Co, solicitors.

'My name is Sampson,' he said to the partner who interviewed him. 'That's right – Sampson – the one you've been reading about. May I sit down?'

Mr Clipper shifted nervously in his seat and said: 'Oh dear!'

He was an admirable solicitor in his own line. If you had a house to sell or wanted to enquire about rights of way or your liability under the Private Streetworks Act, Mr Clipper would serve you very well. Patiently, courteously, skilfully and with no unnecessary delay. But, when it came to what conveyancers consider the more seamy side of the law, litigation or worse, far worse still, crime, he was completely out of his element.

He still remembered that horrible day, many years before Mr Sampson called on him, when he had appeared before the local ogre, His Honour Judge Hoop. Mr Clipper had been called on to take the case at very short notice, owing to the illness of Mr Seaworthy. He had gone to the Court in trepidation fearing the worst, but, fortunately or unfortunately, his imagination before he arrived at Court was wholly unable to do justice to the scene which was to follow. It was infinitely worse than he could possibly have thought.

The judge had not had a good morning and, by the time Mr Clipper's case was reached, he was ready to pounce on everyone and everything. Accordingly Mr Clipper's attempted opening of the facts was punctuated by such interjections from the Bench as: 'That's meaningless,' 'You've said that before,' 'When are you coming to the real issue between the parties?' 'What on earth has this got to do with it?' and other such discouraging remarks. When Mr Clipper referred to the law, unfortunately, owing to his hasty preparation of the case, he got two books mixed up. He had taken nearly a quarter of an hour in reading word for word a case about a tramway collision before he realised with horror that it had nothing whatever to do with the dispute with which he was concerned, namely a claim by a landlord against a tenant.

The judge was interested in law and, knowing that a case of a very different nature from the one which he was trying might have statements about the law in it which were relevant to the case before him, he followed Mr Clipper's reading intently. It is true that, as page followed page without the slightest relevance appearing, he began to wonder, but he still could not believe that there was nothing in the case at all. It was only when Mr Clipper had reached the final paragraph that the judge closed the book with a snap.

'What on earth has this case got to do with it?'

'I'm very sorry, your Honour,' said Mr Clipper miserably, 'I've brought the wrong book.'

He waited for the storm to break. Would it be lightening and thunder? No, it was ice.

'It is hardly less relevant than most of your preceding remarks,' said the judge. 'At least you are consistent, Mr Clipper, in keeping well away from the matters which I have to decide. But no doubt you have a reason – I can't believe that such continuous irrelevance – not to say, if you will forgive me, balderdash – can be without a reason. After all, you're not here for fun. Your client has a case and has paid you to conduct it, and you wouldn't be talking nonsense all the time unless it were in his interests, at least I hope not.'

Mr Clipper remained sorrowfully silent under these insults. As he said nothing the judge went on: 'Well, Mr Clipper, where do we go from here?'

Mr Clipper remembered his first day at boarding school as a very small boy, and the one word that surged through his mind was 'home'. Unfortunately it surged so vigorously that he actually said it.

'And the best place for you, Mr Clipper, if you can't do better than you have so far,' said the judge.

Mr Clipper had had enough. He gathered together his papers, bowed to the judge and left the Court. As he went through the door he heard the judge say: 'Now let's get on.'

He had gone back to his office in a state of utter misery. His partner was ill, which was upsetting enough, and now he had lost one of their best clients. He had been appearing for a man who gave them a great deal of conveyancing work and who was only indulging in a small piece of litigation as a matter of principle. As a landlord he was not going to let his tenant get away with it, no, not if it cost him a couple of hundred pounds. Mr Clipper realised that the winning of the case meant everything to the client, and he would be furious at not only losing it but, as he would rightly be entitled to say, on being let down by his own solicitor. Messrs Weatherstone and Muggeridge would now get all his work

He was sitting in his office some two hours later, with his head between his hands, still wondering whether to tell his partner or wait till he was better, when the client had burst into his room unannounced. At first he thought that he was going to assault him and he reached for the bell, but to his amazement he heard: 'Great work, Clipper.

A master-stroke. Genius, I call it. We'd never have won the case if you'd stayed. But after you'd gone the judge had to do the case for me, and you should have seen what he did to your opponent. Tied him up in knots, threw him up to the ceiling, bounced him on the floor. I thought he was going to leave too. But he hadn't your good sense, Clipper. If he'd gone too, I don't know what would have happened. But he stuck it out, the fool. And we won handsomely. Well done, Clipper, well done. And now we've disposed of that little matter, let's get on with something important. I'm buying a street of houses in Wesmerton. Benchley are the agents. Get on with it for me, my dear fellow, will you.'

Although Mr Clipper had been vastly relieved by his good fortune, he had never, never forgotten his appalling experience before Judge Hoop. Never would he go into Court again. No, not even if his partner were ill, and his best client begged him to go. Perhaps Judge Hoop was not representative of judges as a whole. No matter. He was not going to risk it again. And, whenever a hint of litigation arose in a matter with which he was dealing, he remembered vividly his terrible experience years before.

So, when Mr Sampson said who he was, visions of prison bars, Magistrates' Courts and policemen flashed through Mr Clipper's mind and, behind them, the worst vision of all – Judge Hoop, who had been Chairman of the local Quarter Sessions.

'Er – er – Mr – er Sampson, did you say?' he stammered.

'That's it,' said Mr Sampson cheerfully. 'Mr Clipper, I believe. How d'you do?' and he reached across the desk to shake the solicitor's hand.

'This – er – isn't a police station,' said Mr Clipper. 'Shouldn't you be there?'

'Not if I know it,' said Mr Sampson. 'Let them come to me if they want me. Why should I go to them? I've not disguised myself or grown a moustache or dyed my hair. This is me, Sampson, in the flesh, the man the police want to interview. All right, I say, let them come to me.'

'B–but what can I do for you? I'm afraid I don't do criminal work and my partner, Mr Seaworthy, is away at the moment.'

'Who said criminal work?' asked Mr Sampson.

'B–but blackmail is a crime, a very serious one. I'm not a criminal lawyer myself but I know that much. It's very serious indeed. We don't do that sort of thing, I'm afraid. Now Messrs Weatherstone and Muggeridge in the High Street ...'

'I dare say they're OK,' said Mr Sampson, 'but I've got flat feet, I don't want any more walking and I'd prefer to bring my little bit of business here.'

'And what, may I ask,' stammered Clipper, 'is your little b – bit of b – business?'

'This,' said Mr Sampson, and lifted up a large suitcase. For a moment Clipper wondered if there could be a body in it. Blackmailers were the worst of all criminals. Worse than murderers. After all, a murderer just killed his victim. A blackmailer played him first and then often caused his death later.

'I don't think we can take your case, Mr Sampson,' he said.

'You don't know what it is yet,' said Mr Sampson, and he opened the suitcase. It was full of newspapers.

Mr Clipper was very slightly relieved.

'I don't understand,' he said.

'Look,' said Mr Sampson, and handed him the first paper.

'Blackmailer believed to be in hiding. Search in Chester,' it read.

'Who d'you think that refers to?' asked Mr Sampson.

'Well ... if you'll forgive me,' said Mr Clipper, 'you.'

'Have you any doubt of it?'

'Well – er – no.'

'I shouldn't have forgiven you if you had had any doubt,' said Mr Sampson. 'And these are all the same. I've got a hundred and fifty of them. All the dailies, all the Sundays and lots of provincials. And, just once more, Mr Clipper, who d'you think they refer to?'

'You, Mr Sampson.'

'And you're a reasonable man, Mr Clipper. As a solicitor you must be. Who would any reasonable man think they referred to?'

'Well, you.'

'No doubt at all?'

'None, I'm afraid.'

'But what do they describe me as?'

'A blackmailer, I'm afraid.'

'That's a pretty unpleasant thing to say about anyone, isn't it Mr Clipper?'

'Most unpleasant.'

'What d'you think the damages will be, Mr Clipper?'

'Damages?' said Mr Clipper. 'Damages! There won't be any question of damages, I'm afraid. You're bound to go to prison. They might make you pay the costs as well.'

'You seem to think that I am a blackmailer, Mr Clipper.'

'Well, as you ask me,' said Mr Clipper, 'I do.'

'Why?'

'Well – all this,' and Mr Clipper pointed to the newspapers.

'Splendid,' said Mr Sampson. 'That's what everyone would say, isn't it? I'm convicted before I'm tried, aren't I?'

'Oh, no, Mr Sampson. I assure you, you'll get a perfectly fair trial before you're convicted.'

'You don't think all this might prejudice the jury a bit?'

'The judge will tell them it mustn't.'

'Well, that's very comforting,' said Mr Sampson, 'if they take any notice of the judge.'

'Oh, they will, I'm sure.'

'Well, I don't share your confidence about that, but never mind. Suppose I'm not guilty? Suppose the whole thing's a stupid mistake? Or suppose it were an attempt by someone to make money out of *me*? Suppose, for any reason you like, that I'm not a blackmailer – what about these newspapers then? Can people say that about me if it isn't true?'

Mr Clipper thought for a moment.

'Well, I don't personally know much about these things, but I believe there is something called fair comment.'

'What! Fair comment to call an innocent man a blackmailer. The law can't be as stupid as that.'

'No, I suppose not,' said Mr Clipper. 'To call you a blackmailer is more a statement of fact than a comment.'

'Well, then, suppose I'm not – what are the damages likely to be?'

'You mean if you sued them for libel?'

'Exactly.'

'Well, I don't really deal with such matters myself, but from what I've read I suppose they'd be quite large. But that's only if it isn't true.'

'Tell me, Mr Clipper, do I look like a blackmailer?'

'Well, quite frankly,' said Mr Clipper, 'I've never seen one before to my knowledge.'

'Careful, Mr Clipper, careful,' said Mr Sampson. 'You said "before," and, if there'd been someone else present, you'd be for it too, wouldn't you? It's all right,' he added, as he saw the anxious look on Mr Clipper's face, 'I want help from you, not damages, and anyway there wasn't anyone else present, unless you've got someone listening in and, as you didn't know I was coming, that's unlikely, unless you do it for every client.'

'No one else heard it, I assure you,' said Mr Clipper.

'But, of course,' said Mr Sampson, 'to call a man a blackmailer is quite insulting, isn't it? And it might make the other chap want to hit you on the nose. All of which adds up to conduct likely to provoke a breach of the peace. Now, don't worry, Mr Clipper, I shan't prefer a charge. You're my solicitor, aren't you, and you're going to act for me. It would be base ingratitude to bring you along to the police court. And it wouldn't do anyone any good, would it? "Local Solicitor Charged," or even "Local Solicitor Acquitted." Wouldn't look good at all, would it? Now let's get on with my little matter. I want you to write a letter to all these newspapers.'

'But surely,' said Mr Clipper, 'you ought to give yourself up first?'

'Give myself up?' asked Mr Sampson, 'What for?'

'For – er – er – alleged blackmail.'

'That isn't an offence, Mr Clipper – not *alleged* blackmail; only blackmail. Why should I give myself up for that if I'm not guilty?'

'Well, the police have asked you to.'

'Why should I do what the police ask? I'm not driving a car and being asked to stop or slow down or keep to a particular line of traffic. I tell you, I'm not hiding. I'm simply not calling on them.'

'Then would you mind if I told them where you were?'

'I most certainly would, Mr Clipper. I'm not a criminal – and you certainly don't know that I am – and I'm not concealing my identity. I just don't choose to assist the police in this particular matter. For one thing I never have liked their methods. And, as I've come to you in confidence, Mr Clipper, I should certainly go to Messrs

Weatherstone and Muggeridge if you broke that confidence. No doubt a solicitor mustn't conceal or abet a man whom he knows to be on the run, but you don't know anything about me, except what you've read in the papers, and I tell you that it's quite untrue that I'm a blackmailer and I can prove it. Right. Shall we get on with the letters?'

'To whom d'you wish me to write?'

'To whom? The whole lot, of course.'

'And *what* do you wish me to write?'

'Well, I'll suggest the effect of the letters. You can put it into solicitors' language. Perhaps you'd better have your secretary in. Then there *will* be a third party present.'

Somewhat reluctantly Mr Clipper sent for Miss Pink.

' "We have been consulted by our client, Mr Richard Sampson," ' Mr Sampson began when she was ready, ' " … by Mr Richard Sampson of" … of – I don't think we'll put in an address for the moment – "in regard to a very serious libel published by you about our client in your issue of the" – fill in that according to the newspaper, in some cases you'll find there are several issues. "Our client is amazed that a newspaper of your standing should, without any knowledge of the true facts, publish such a scandalous libel upon our client. This is calculated to ruin our client and accordingly, unless you publish with equally large prominence a complete withdrawal and apology within forty-eight hours of receipt of this letter, proceedings will follow. Although the damage to our client is enormous he will not at this stage require damages for himself if you take every step to remedy the wrong you have done him but, to mark the gravity of the matter, he will also require you to make a substantial payment to charity."

'Then put in any charity you like. As for the amount, put in £1,000 for the nationals and £100 for the provincials. Then wind up by saying proceedings will be taken at once if these terms are not complied with. Oh – of course, say I'll want my costs as well. Which reminds me. You don't know me, except, shall we say, by reputation. So you'd rather have something on account? I thought you mightn't at this stage care for a cheque. So here's fifty pounds in cash on account. I'll be back to hear the answers in three or four days. But, don't forget, if I find the police waiting for me, I know where to find Messrs Weatherstone and Muggeridge. Now, if there's nothing else you want, I'll be on my way. Good morning.'

'Was that really Sampson?' asked Miss Pink, after he had gone.

'Well, I believe so,' said Mr Clipper, 'but we've only his word for it. It might be a practical joker, I suppose. Why didn't I think of that before? I knew I shouldn't have taken on the case. But he made me, really he did. He pretty well blackmailed me into it. Now what have I said? Don't repeat that on any account, Miss Pink.'

'Are you going to tell the police?' she asked.

'No, not at present,' said Mr Clipper. 'As a matter of fact, I think these letters should do the trick. The whole of the Press will be down here. They'll soon find him, if Scotland Yard don't. Let's get on with them. First of all make me a list of all the newspapers with their addresses.'

A few days later the editors and proprietors of a hundred and fifty newspapers received a letter from Messrs Seaworthy, Clipper and Co. They at once consulted solicitors, some of them separately, some of them together.

'Of all the impudence!' said one editor and that was the general conclusion. It was obviously an attempt either to ward off prosecution or to make it more difficult. In consequence all the letters which were sent in reply were similar to this:

> We duly received your letter of the 15th instant. Our clients are amazed at the effrontery of a man who is hiding from the police. We suggest that, instead of making ludicrous demands upon our clients, your client who, we note, does not disclose his address, gives himself up to the police at the earliest possible moment. None of your client's demands will be complied with and we will accept service of any proceedings which your client may be bold enough to instruct you to begin. In this connection may we remind you that the address of the plaintiff must appear on a writ and we are sure we can rely on you to make certain that it is a genuine one.

Mr Sampson duly called on Mr Clipper and was shown the replies.

'Right,' he said, 'kindly issue writs against every one of them. I've brought some more money to pay for the fees. Will £500 be enough?'

'Yes, thank you,' said Mr Clipper, rather surprised. 'But what about the address?'

'I'm staying at the Bull at Maiseley. Don't look so doubtful. You can ring them up if you like and check on me. Or come and dine with me there tonight. Better still, come and dine the day after they get these writs. There'll be quite a crowd there, I should imagine. In replying you might mention that I have not been hiding anywhere, but that I have been staying, in my own name, at the Bull where the police or any party interested can find me.'

Mr Sampson went back to the Bull and had a word with the proprietor.

'I don't know how many you usually cater for, but, if I were you, I should have enough lunches for a hundred at least on Friday.'

'Why on earth?' asked the landlord.

'Well, don't say that I didn't warn you,' replied Mr Sampson.

CHAPTER TWENTY-ONE

Culsworth Cross-Examined

In the meantime Mr Baker's case had been going on. After he had completed his evidence the defendant's case was opened and the defendant himself was called. He was a far more ordinary witness than Mr Baker, but much more shifty and he did not make a good impression. Finally Culsworth was called.

As he walked into the witness box he tried not to think of the effect which his evidence might have upon the future of himself and his family, but he could not avoid a feeling of sickening fear. He took the oath, was asked the usual formal questions, and then the important one.

'Did Mr Baker ever tell you of a conversation he had with the defendant after the litigation had started?'

'No.'

'Are you sure?'

'As sure as one can be.'

'Did he tell you that the defendant pretty well admitted liability, but said the plaintiff couldn't prove it?'

'Nothing of the kind.'

'Are you sure?'

'As sure as one can be.'

'But if he had told you anything of the sort would you have remembered it?'

'Almost certainly.'

'Almost?'

'Well, I'm sure I should have.'

'Thank you, Mr Culsworth.'

Panter then rose to cross-examine. This was the moment. Was he going to attack him as a liar would be attacked? Or merely attack his recollection. If the Moriarty case were going to be put to him, surely it must be the former? But you can never be sure. And Panter was a suave cross-examiner. He seldom, if ever, appeared to attack the witness. He was always courteous and would, as it were, take the most hostile witness by the hand to lead him into the path of truth rather than by the throat to choke it out of him. How would he begin?

'I suppose you think it's a pretty serious thing to throw up a case in the middle, Mr Culsworth?'

Oh, God! I don't like this, thought Culsworth.

'Yes, of course,' he said.

'Have you ever done it before?'

'Only on one occasion.'

'Because your client lied?'

'Not exactly. I became satisfied that he'd put up a false case.'

'Was this while you were on your feet or when you had time to consider the matter? I mean, for example, during an adjournment.'

'It was during an adjournment.'

'In the case of Mr Baker, it was in Court?'

'Yes.'

'Rather on the spur of the moment?'

Oh, God! He's leading to it.

'Not exactly on the spur of the moment. I was not on my feet.'

'Then you recognise you might make a mistake on the spur of the moment?'

It's nice of him to call it a mistake, but I can't. This is it. But there must be a few more questions first.

'Yes, one could make a mistake,' said Culsworth.

'And you didn't have much time in the present case to think about it?'

'No.'

'Couldn't you have taken a little longer to decide? After all, the man was your client.'

'But I was sure.'

'As sure as you could be you mean, don't you?'

'Well, yes.'

'That means there might be room for mistake. We all make mistakes, do we not?'

'Of course.'

'That includes you?'

'Naturally.'

'Have you never in the course of a case said something too quickly and it turned out to be wrong?'

Turned out to be wrong! That was an odd way of putting it, thought Culsworth. It *was* wrong and he knew it. But, of course, there were other occasions where he had just made a mistake. Well, that was all he was asked at the moment.

'Yes, certainly.'

Don't please ask me if I've always corrected it, Culsworth prayed. But he's bound to. I thought for the moment that he might be on another tack altogether. But of course not. This is Panter's way. He's going to make me convict myself or lie. What a perfect way of cross-examining a colleague. None of the 'I put it to you that you did so-and-so,' or even 'I'm sorry to have to put this to you but didn't you etc. etc.' Nothing of the kind. Just gentle questions which force the convicting answer from the witness.

'Don't you think you could have been wrong in the present case?' went on Panter.

'I could have been, I suppose, but I wasn't.'

This was better. Could he possibly be leading to something quite different?

'But isn't a mistake more likely to be made if you act so quickly? More likely than if you give it several minutes thought?'

'I suppose so.'

This is wonderful. He's not leading to Moriarty. Surely he can't be.

'So in the present case,' continued Panter, 'you were more likely to make a mistake than if you'd thought about it for longer?'

'Yes.'

'More likely than in the other case from which you withdrew?'

'Yes.'

'It was in fact only a similar sort of time interval as in the cases where you've made a mistake?'

Is this leading back to Moriarty?

'I suppose so.'

'So this could be another of them?'

He isn't on Moriarty. He can't be or he'd have come to it this time surely.

'It could,' said Culsworth.

'Let's see if it was.'

Relief poured through Culsworth's body. He now felt almost certain that he was safe. He could hardly wait for the next question, for the more he was cross-examined without Moriarty being mentioned the surer he would be that he was safe.

'Your client said in evidence that at an interview at a public house after the writ had been issued the defendant impliedly admitted his liability, didn't he?'

'Yes.'

'He also said, didn't he, that he didn't attach much importance to it as he was the only person who heard it?'

'Yes.'

'Was that quite reasonable for him in your view?'

'Not unreasonable.'

'So that it was the sort of thing he might either not mention or not stress?'

'I suppose so.'

'Or he might mention part of it and not mention the other?'

'How d'you mean?' Culsworth asked.

He was so overjoyed at what looked like his complete safety that he was really anxious to help the cross-examiner.

'Well, as he attached little or no importance to the matter, he might have casually mentioned that he saw the defendant in a public house and not bothered to say what happened. After all, his attitude of mind was "It's word against word. If I'm not believed on the original promise I shan't be believed about this either. So what does it matter?" That's reasonable, isn't it?'

'Yes, I should say so.'

'Now, if your client had only said to you that he'd seen the defendant in a public house, without telling you about the conversation, that would have made no impression on you at all, would it? It would have been completely immaterial.'

'Yes, that is so.'

'So that, if all the plaintiff said to you was that, you might well either not have registered it or, if you did actually take it in, you might have forgotten it?'

'Yes,' replied Culsworth, 'that's possible.'

'Well, then, you can't swear, can you, that the plaintiff didn't tell you he'd seen the defendant in a public house?'

'No, I can't swear he didn't say just that.'

'Let us then assume,' proceeded Panter, 'that he did say it. After all, he swears that he did say it and you can't swear that he didn't. That's right, isn't it?'

'Yes.'

'Now, if he did say just that he'd seen the defendant in a public house, but didn't attach any more importance to that fact than he attached to the conversation that took place, it's not unreasonable that, as he did mention the one fact, he might have *thought* he mentioned the other fact too, even if he didn't mention it.'

'Yes, that's fair.'

'Well, if that's fair, don't you think you were a little hasty in throwing up the case as in effect you did? Your client may well have told you half the story and thought he'd told you the whole story. There's nothing dishonest about that, is there?'

'Nothing at all,' agreed Culsworth.

'Then, I repeat, don't you think you may have done your client an injustice by getting up as you did, with so little time for thought, and saying, as in effect you did, that your client was telling lies?'

Culsworth thought for a moment or two.

'I think you're probably right,' he said. 'I think I may owe my client a profound apology.'

'Thank you, Mr Culsworth,' said Panter. 'That is all I wish to ask.'

And indeed there was nothing left for him to ask.

Apart from Culsworth's evidence, the case had gone very well from Mr Baker's point of view, and now Panter had completely neutralised that evidence. Even the judge, in summing up to the jury, suggested that they might well think that they need not concern themselves with that matter. The sole question was, who was telling the truth. The jury decided that it was Mr Baker, and he obtained judgment for his £15,000.

Later on, when he was thanking Panter for his services, the latter said to him: 'Now, Mr Baker, d'you see how foolish it would have been to suggest that Mr Culsworth was a liar? He was nothing of the kind. You or he, or both of you, made a mistake that's all. If I'd done what you wanted you'd probably have lost the case.'

'Well,' said Mr Baker, 'we all make mistakes and I agree I was wrong. I'm most grateful to you. It's meant a lot to me as you can imagine. Mr Culsworth can't be feeling so good, though.'

But Culsworth was feeling very good indeed, and when he telephoned the good news to his wife he was so emotionally affected that he could hardly speak on the telephone. There was, of course, still the possibility that Mr Sampson would make further attempts on him but, as he had seen fit to disappear, the danger was infinitely less.

CHAPTER TWENTY-TWO

Mr Sampson Assists the Police

The day after the writs had been received by the various newspapers' solicitors, there was, as Mr Sampson had anticipated, a large gathering at the Bull at Maiseley. The police and journalists arrived simultaneously. Mr Sampson courteously but firmly refused to make any statement to the Press, but he agreed to see the police officers. They suggested it would be more convenient if they went to the nearest police station. Mr Sampson said that he didn't agree.

'Of course, if you're arresting me, I'll do what I'm told. Couldn't very well do anything else. But otherwise I'll help you in your enquiries from here or not at all. Which is it to be?'

'We are not arresting you at present,' said the inspector.

'Then here it is or not at all,' said Mr Sampson. 'Now, how can I help you?'

'Complaints have been made by a lady called Mrs Verney that you have been blackmailing her. I'd like to put her statement to you and see to what extent, if any, you agree with her.'

'That's fair enough,' said Mr Sampson, 'but let me make this plain at once, I have not been blackmailing her or anyone else.'

'Very well then,' said the inspector. 'Do you agree that you've been going to see her?'

'Yes.'

'Why?'

'In the course of business.'

'What business?'

'I'm an enquiry agent.'

'What were you investigating?'

'Will you keep this confidential?'

'Well, that depends,' said the inspector. 'Anything you now say may be used in evidence if you're prosecuted, but, if you're not prosecuted, I'll undertake that this information won't go beyond the police and the Director of Public Prosecutions' office.'

'That's fair enough,' said Mr Sampson. 'Well, I was employed by her husband, who suspected that she'd been unfaithful to him.'

'She says that you threatened that, unless she paid you at least a hundred pounds, you'd tell her husband about her.'

'Certainly not. Money never came into it. Certainly I told her all sorts of things to get information out of her, but I never suggested that she should pay me a penny. After I'd found out as much as I thought I could, I let on who I was. I think she'd guessed it anyway. Then she tried to bribe *me*. Not in so many words, but by hints. You know the sort of thing I mean.'

'She says that you told her you'd bought information about her going with a man to the Fisherman's Nook Hotel from an organisation which sells such information.'

'Well, there's something in that. There is an organisation which I use when I'm making enquiries, and they do buy information from chambermaids and so forth. Then they sell it on to us.'

'What is this organisation? Who runs it?'

'That I'm not telling,' said Mr Sampson. 'It's a condition of getting the information that we don't disclose where we got it from. There's nothing illegal about it, but it's not a nice sort of trade and they like to remain anonymous. So I'm not saying.'

The inspector continued to question Mr Sampson about his interviews with Margaret, but he got no information from him which would have corroborated her story, except that the actual interviews were admitted and some parts of the conversations. But Mr Sampson admitted nothing which would have been corroboration of her evidence that he was blackmailing her. The inspector then dealt with Mr Sampson's other behaviour in the Temple, except for his interview with Culsworth – of which he was unaware. Mr Sampson substantially admitted that he had been going round the Temple making enquiries of one kind and another. It was simply because he thought he might get information which would assist him in his work as an enquiry agent. Why had he run away? He'd done nothing of the kind. He wanted a short holiday. When he saw the attack on him in the newspapers he did not go to a police station because he saw no earthly reason why he should. He wanted a peaceful holiday and he certainly wouldn't get that with journalists all around him. That was inevitable now, but he'd put off the evil day as long as he could.

After a conversation lasting several hours, the police officers told Mr Sampson that they would report the result of the interview to their superiors. Would Mr Sampson undertake not to leave the country or disappear?

'Really,' said Mr Sampson, 'this is too bad. I will give no undertaking of any kind. You can always communicate with me through my solicitors, whose name and address you know. I will go where I like and when I like, and I shan't ask the police for their permission.'

'Mr Sampson,' said the inspector, 'you're quite entitled to adopt that attitude if you wish. But is it wise? Suppose you are arrested, questions of bail may arise, and I should be bound to report what you said at this interview and to oppose bail because of it.'

'If you arrest me,' said Mr Sampson, 'you'll oppose bail anyway.'

'Not necessarily,' said the inspector.

'Well, I shall take a chance of that. I'm giving no undertakings.'

The police officers had to be satisfied with that and they duly reported the result of the interview. The evidence was considered in the office of the Director of Public Prosecutions. An officer went to see Margaret and put to her what Sampson had said.

'What I've told you is the truth,' she said. 'And as for Edward employing an enquiry agent, it's nonsense. If he'd been in the least suspicious I'd have known it. Besides, if he'd known about the Fisherman's Nook, what more did he want? Thank God he doesn't, but you won't speak to him, will you, or he may.'

The officer said he would report to his superiors what she had said.

CHAPTER TWENTY-THREE

Legal Proceedings

Prosecutions for serious offences in this country are not lightly undertaken. Very occasionally, one suspects, a charge is made although the making of it is against the better judgment of those responsible for deciding whether it should be made or not. Such rare occurrences take place, if at all, because it is considered that the harm done by an unsuccessful prosecution would be less than the harm done by the public outcry at the absence of a prosecution. Sometimes, as in the case of Mr Sampson, things get out of hand and so many rumours find their way into print that the public expects a prosecution as soon as the man or woman is found. Indeed they do not discuss his guilt or innocence, but only the penalty which should be imposed.

On the other hand, the authorities will not normally be dragooned into a prosecution when it would be bound to fail. They consider first and foremost what evidence there is that a crime has been committed. If there is no reasonable evidence to lay before a magistrate or a jury, then no prosecution will be undertaken, and if complaint were made in the House of Commons the Attorney-General would explain to the House that no case could be made out. On the other hand, if there is evidence to sustain a conviction the next question normally considered is whether a conviction is likely to be obtained upon that evidence. It is in the cases where the chances of securing a conviction are either small or no more than even that the difficulty arises. In such cases both the public good and the rights of the individual have to be considered most carefully. The Director of Public Prosecutions is not going to put a man through the horror of a criminal trial just because he knows the public would like it. On the other hand, in a borderline case, if it appears to be strongly in the public interest that the matter should be ventilated in Court, the private interest of the person concerned may have to be subordinated to the public good.

Mr Sampson's case was a peculiarly difficult one. He was, as far as was known, a man of good character, and if, on a criminal trial it was simply a case of his word against Margaret's with no corroboration of her story, any jury would be almost bound to acquit, particularly as Margaret would have to admit that she had deceived her husband. Even if the jury preferred her evidence to Sampson's that would not be enough. They would have to be satisfied beyond all reasonable doubt that she was telling the truth and he was telling lies. There was, however, one possible way of corroborating Margaret's story. Sampson had said that he was employed by her husband as an enquiry agent. If this were untrue, why should he say it if he were innocent?

But the difficulty was this. If what Mr Sampson had said was true, then he would obviously be acquitted. Indeed, if at an interview Edward Verney corroborated his story, Mr Sampson would not be prosecuted. If, however, what Mr Sampson said was untrue, and the fact was that Edward Verney knew nothing of the Fisherman's Nook, the only

145

method of proving the untruth would be to call Edward as a witness, which would disclose to him the very fact which enabled Mr Sampson to blackmail his wife. It was true that the public interest might require the prosecution of a blackmailer, even at the expense of his victim, but if any other course were open which would protect the victim it was obviously desirable to take it. Few victims of blackmail go to the police. Hardly any would go if they thought they would be given away by the police themselves.

Fortunately Mr Sampson's own action in issuing writs against the newspaper proprietors showed the Director's office the way out of the difficulty. During the course of these actions the truth about Edward Verney would almost certainly be disclosed. If it were not, the matter could be reconsidered. If the jury in the civil actions found that Mr Sampson was a blackmailer, a prosecution could reasonably be undertaken, even if it failed eventually because of the higher measure of proof required in a criminal case. On the other hand, if Mr Sampson were successful, obviously there could be no prosecution. The important thing, from the Director's point of view, was that the matter was going to be ventilated in open Court. If Mr Sampson had not started his civil proceedings, it would have been much more difficult to arrive at a decision. As those responsible for making this decision were lawyers the public might think that, if no proceedings of any kind took place, they were trying to protect their colleagues and hush up the whole affair.

So it was decided to postpone a decision on prosecution until after the hearing of Mr Sampson's actions. Of course, if he withdrew them before trial, a decision would have to be taken then. It was appreciated that Mr Sampson's object in issuing the writs might be to delay or avoid prosecution, but, even if that were the case, the difficulties of proof were such that it seemed better to let him have this temporary advantage rather than to start a prosecution at that stage. There was, too, the advantage that the rules in civil cases were far less strict, and it might be possible to cross-examine Mr Sampson about his behaviour in the Temple. This might be impossible in a criminal case.

The decision not to prosecute (if at all) until after the conclusion of the civil proceedings, was conveyed to the solicitors acting for the newspapers. Naturally they were not pleased, but it was an intelligible decision, and they now had to consider what evidence they could call if Mr Sampson were bold enough to bring the actions to trial which, at that stage, they doubted very much. To save costs and time all the newspapers decided to be represented by one firm of solicitors, and they appointed a small committee who would instruct the solicitors on the course they should take. In the event of a disagreement among the committee, a meeting of all the defendants would be convened.

The first thing to be done was to interview Margaret and to see what kind of a witness she would make. Mr Springfold, the senior partner in the defendants' solicitors, interviewed her himself and came to the conclusion that she would make an excellent witness. He satisfied himself that substantially everything she said had happened as she said it had happened. But he could also see that, reasonably enough, she was terrified that the resultant publicity would make her identity known to her husband. Mr Springfold promised that neither his firm nor the defendants would communicate with her husband, but he recommended her to employ solicitors of her own to protect her interests, and, he added, he felt sure the defendants would pay her costs. She gladly accepted the offer and was introduced to Messrs Tracery, Skane and Lutt.

'You do see,' she said to Mr Lutt, 'that it is absolutely vital that my husband should not know anything.'

'Of course,' said Mr Lutt. 'I feel sure that the Court will let you be known as Mrs X.'

'Could I refuse to give evidence if the judge wouldn't agree to that?'

'No, I'm afraid you couldn't. But I can't think that any judge would be so unfair as to refuse permission.'

'Then what about photographs?'

'They can't take photographs in or as you go into the Court and, anyway, it will be my job to see that you are protected and fully protected throughout the proceedings.'

'What sort of questions will I be asked?'

'You'll simply be asked to tell your story in the first instance. Then, no doubt, Mr Sampson's counsel will try to make you alter it and will put to you his client's version of the interviews.'

'Will I be asked about the Fisherman's Nook Hotel?'

'I'm afraid you will, but I feel sure that the judge will allow the name to be written down.'

'Will I be asked about the man I went with?'

'Yes, but again I'm sure you'll be allowed to write the name down. And don't forget this too, the whole of the Press are on your side. So it's in the highest degree improbable that anything will be done to embarrass you. On the contrary I feel certain that all the newspapers will give an undertaking that everything will be done to protect you. You're really in a very strong position, Mrs Verney. You are virtually the sole witness for the defendants. If you let them down, they'll be sunk. So it's to their interest to do all they can to help you.'

'You've relieved my mind a great deal,' said Margaret, 'but there's always the possibility that my husband may find out accidentally. For example, if he had 'flu or something when I was going to Court.'

'Well, there is one thing I must warn you about, Mrs Verney, but, subject to this one warning, I think you'll be safe. Now I believe you to be telling the truth, so do the defendants. But suppose we're wrong, suppose Mr Sampson is employed as an enquiry agent by your husband, he may be called as a witness at the trial by the plaintiff. The defendants have promised not to contact him, but Mr Sampson may.'

'But that's ridiculous,' said Margaret. 'If Edward knew about the Fisherman's Nook he'd have let me know years ago. I know Edward. No, Mr Sampson won't bring my husband to the Court. It'd prove him to be a liar.'

'Good. Then for the rest, I think you'll find the defendants will give you all the help you need. They've got some pretty good brains among them and I'm morally certain that, if we tell them what the difficulty is, they'll find a way out. For example – this is only a sudden thought – they could say you'd won a snap beauty competition. You know the sort of thing, girls snapped in the Street, and they could then invite you to stay at an hotel for a couple of days or so as one of the winners. Those days would, of course, correspond with the trial. You'd get all the publicity from the so-called beauty competition and no one would know you were really the chief witness in Mr Sampson's case. Now I only made up that on the spur of the moment. I'm sure there are a hundred and one things which could be arranged. And you're in what I think is a historically unique position, you've got the entire Press behind you. I expect you'd like me to have a chat with Mr Springfold about it all?'

'Thank you. I would indeed.'

So Mr Lutt and Mr Springfold got together and between them, with the help of some of the more imaginative of the journalists, they evolved plans to ensure Margaret's anonymity before and during the trial. They did all this before the time for the delivery of the defence had arrived. From the defendants' point of view this was very important. Although they could compel Margaret to give evidence, whether she wanted to or not, and although she did not appear to be a person who would deliberately tell untruths, there is a world of difference between a willing, helpful witness and a reluctant one. In cross-examination the latter may all too easily be persuaded to say that he 'does not remember,' or 'isn't quite sure,' or that 'perhaps he was mistaken, it was a long time ago,' or, if a witness on the other side says so-and-so, that 'he is not actually prepared to say that that witness is lying,' and so on.

In consequence of Mr Springfold's and Mr Lutt's efforts, it was unanimously agreed that the defence would be that Mr Sampson had demanded money from Margaret with menaces and without reasonable or probable cause. Although the libels complained of also referred in obviously defamatory terms to Mr Sampson's behaviour in the Temple, and although that part of the libel could not be justified, the defendants' legal advisers were quite satisfied that, if the jury accepted Margaret's story, the damages would be negligible. They paid £100 into court to deal with that side of the case. This meant that, if the jury awarded that sum or less in respect of these other libels, Mr Sampson would have the whole of the costs of the actions to pay. Nor could anyone conceive that, if the jury said that Mr Sampson had blackmailed Margaret, they would award anything worth speaking of for the other libels. £100 was an outside figure, in case there was someone on the jury who objected to the Press pinning, say, six murders on a man when he'd only committed one.

While the action was proceeding, Mr Sampson remained at Maiseley, and regularly went to see his solicitors to see how things were going on. Mr Clipper had by this time handed the matter over to Mr Seaworthy.

'They're justifying,' said Mr Seaworthy, on one of Mr Sampson's visits. 'You will remember that I told you that would happen. But they're only relying on the Verney episode. That means they've got no evidence from the Temple. They've paid £100 into Court.'

'Say I'm not interested.'

'It's not necessary. Unless you accept it, it's automatically taken to be refused.'

'Good,' said Mr Sampson. 'Now, how much am I likely to get?'

'Mr Sampson,' said Mr Seaworthy, 'I hope you're not underrating your opponents. You've the whole of the Press lined up against you.'

'I hope they're not underrating me. As far as I can see, I've only Margaret Verney lined up against me.'

'That's true in a sense. But you'll be cross-examined by the finest brains at the Bar.'

'That should be an interesting experience. But, as Mrs Verney is really the only witness against me, what would happen if she were run into by a 'bus?'

'It might be possible for her statements to be read out.'

'Well, suppose she disappeared?'

'The same probably.'

'But you can't cross-examine a statement.'

'That's true, nor is it on oath. If she died, the jury would pay more attention to her statement than if she disappeared.'

'Well, why not offer her £100 or something to disappear?'

'I hope you're not serious, Mr Sampson, because, if you are, I'm afraid you'll have to find another solicitor to take the case.'

'Of course not,' said Mr Sampson. 'But how much d'you think the Press are going to pay her?'

'I can only say that I am quite certain she will not have been promised anything, except her expenses. I quite agree that, if they win the case, they may make her a present but, if they're wise, no one will even have hinted at that.'

'Just as a matter of interest, Mr Seaworthy, tell me this. If the defendants may pay her the expenses of giving evidence, why should it be wrong for me to pay her the expenses of not giving evidence? Now, please don't get indignant. I assure you I shan't do anything without your advice. It just seemed odd to me that they could do the one thing if I can't do the other.'

'To prevent a witness from giving evidence by a bribe is tampering with the due administration of justice. To pay the expenses necessarily incurred by a witness is doing nothing of the kind.'

'It all depends what the expenses are.'

'Of course. To pay a witness £1,000 for giving evidence would be a bribe.'

'Suppose the witness were abroad and wouldn't come without it?'

'That would be different. A witness couldn't be compelled to come over here from abroad and, provided the amount paid were disclosed, there would be nothing improper in the transaction. A witness in this country can be compelled to give evidence, and to pay or promise such a witness more than proper expenses would be improper.

I'm not, of course, referring to expert witnesses who can demand their own fees.'

'Well, thank you for all that information,' said Mr Sampson. 'Now, let's get back to the damages. What are your views?'

'If the jury believe Mrs Verney, there won't be any damages, none worth speaking of. That's what the £100 is for.'

'And why shouldn't they believe me and not her?'

'You should know that better than I, Mr Sampson. My own view is that, if you're telling the truth, the jury will believe you, and *vice versa*.'

'And if you were on the jury?'

'I haven't seen or heard Mrs Verney.'

'Well, I'd say she'd be a good witness. How d'you think I'll do?'

'Well, if I may say so, Mr Sampson, you have plenty of confidence. That could be a help or a hindrance. You'll be seeing your counsel in due course and no doubt he will give you good advice, but, if you take my advice, you won't be too jaunty in the box. Juries are apt to dislike or suspect too obviously self-satisfied witnesses.'

'You're very frank.'

'That's one of the things you pay me for.'

'Well, who's going to win?'

'I really don't know, but, if you insist on my giving you my instinctive feelings on the matter – which may well be wrong – I think *they* will.'

'You're frightened of the big battalions, Mr Seaworthy. That's it, isn't it? Or perhaps you're frightened of me? That only shows the harm the newspapers can do. You read all about me before I came here, and you can't get the first flavour out of your mouth.'

'There's something in that, Mr Sampson – but ... I take it you still want me to be frank?'

'Of course.'

'Well – in that case – you have done nothing to get rid of the first flavour – on the contrary, your behaviour with Mr Clipper confirmed it.'

'You think I'm a blackmailer, then?'

'Quite frankly I think you may be.'

'It's lucky a solicitor doesn't have to believe in his client.'

'If you'd like to take the case elsewhere, Mr Sampson, I shall fully understand.'

'Shouldn't dream of it, Mr Seaworthy. I like frankness. It's much too rare. I'm sure there are plenty of solicitors who'd have answered my question by saying: "Good heavens, no, Mr Sampson, I'm quite sure you're a gentleman of complete integrity but unfortunately the case doesn't depend on my view and, although the jury ought to take the same view as I do, they don't know you as well, and might not." Confounded hypocrites. I bet they say that to dozens of chaps who're as guilty as they can be and whom they're jolly well sure are guilty.'

'Well, Mr Sampson, it's most refreshing to have a client who appreciates these things.'

'But I still want an answer to my question. Suppose your instincts are all wrong and I'm believed and Mrs Verney isn't, what'll the damages be?'

'I can only say astronomic,' said Mr Seaworthy. 'You've been described by all the defendants, in some cases with lurid untrue details, as a dangerous blackmailer. Their defence is that you are one. If that defence fails the defendants will have to pay a vast sum of damages altogether. No one can be certain of these things, but I should say at least £100,000 – and that's under £1,000 each. No, Mr Sampson, if you're the person of integrity you claim to be you're going to make a lot of money. And it will be free of tax.'

'Now, that's very pleasant hearing,' said Mr Sampson. 'That's the nicest thing you've said since we met. I think I shall go home on that note. £100,000. Very nice. I should sleep well tonight.'

'But, if you lose, you will almost certainly be prosecuted and you may get the maximum sentence if convicted.'

'Why spoil my dreams? And you sound quite cheerful at the thought of my losing. It's lucky you don't have to like your clients. And *vice versa*. Good morning.'

CHAPTER TWENTY-FOUR

Preparations for Trial

One evening not long before Mr Sampson's case came on for trial, Culsworth and his wife were discussing the matter. They were now pretty confident that Culsworth would not be involved, but nothing could be certain until the trial was over, or indeed after that, if Mr Sampson chose to pursue the matter.

'What I can't understand,' said Culsworth, 'is why he ever approached me unless he was going to do something about it. He can't have mentioned Moriarty by accident. He must have been told what happened in that case. He makes no demand on me of any kind, just shows that he knows, goes away, and never comes back. What on earth is his object?'

'I suppose it's possible,' said Jane, 'that he does one thing at a time. That he wanted to finish his transaction with Mrs Verney first and was merely preparing the ground for approaching you later. Then I suppose things got too hot for him and he cleared out. What d'you yourself make of the libel action?'

'A try-on if ever there was one. A spectacular one, mark you, because, if Margaret Verney comes to grief in the witness box, the damages would be fantastic. But she won't come to grief. Of course the jury won't know, as I know, that she's telling the truth, but I'm quite certain that she'll convince them without difficulty. Mr Sampson's a smart alec who may amuse them but, when it comes to comparing their stories, I'm sure hers will stand out as the true one. Of course, it's dangerous to rely on one witness only, but in this case there's no one else they could call. Except me, I suppose, if I told them the truth.'

'But he never asked you for money.'

'No, but what else could his object have been? If I told the defendants that Mr Sampson was on a good thing when he mentioned Moriarty, they could rely on his mentioning the name as the first step in blackmail. But this would only be valuable if I admitted what had happened in Moriarty's case. And, whether I'm right or wrong, I'm not going to disclose that to save all the Press in England. Perhaps I should, but I shan't. If I needed convincing, what you said to me to try to make me lie again has satisfied me that I needn't voluntarily commit suicide. Of course Mr Sampson may come to me again, but, when he's lost these actions, I expect he'll be prosecuted and, although he might still get off – for lack of proof I mean – I think he'll be a bit careful about going any further with it.'

'Suppose he wins?'

'In that case he'll be so rich that I can't imagine even a confirmed criminal risking his life or his liberty again. But he won't win. I know Margaret Verney. I've heard her tell her story from the start. And if she wasn't telling me almost word for word something which had actually happened, then I'm not the judge of character which some of my clients think I am.'

It will be seen that both experienced lawyers, Culsworth and Springfold, came to exactly the same conclusion. That does not mean that experienced lawyers are always right, however confident they may be, but in the present case there was in fact no doubt that Margaret had described her interviews with Mr Sampson almost exactly as they had happened. It was not, therefore, surprising that she was believed.

The defendants had briefed two counsel who were recognised to be at the top of their profession. Sir Maxwell Fawcett was the leader and Enton Hall the junior. The latter was briefed in practically every libel action and he knew more on the subject than anyone else at the Bar. Indeed he knew more about it than many of the judges. He had specialised in the subject for thirty years and he had a top-class brain. Fawcett was a common law leader who was a most powerful advocate. Just the sort of man to crush a blackmailer. Although not of the old Marshall Hall school, he had something of that school about him, and it was worth while listening to him knocking his opponent round the ring without mercy, not so much in cross-examination, where the witness could knock back, but in addressing a jury where, within certain limits, he could say what he liked. Many a witness who found him a courteous cross-examiner changed his view of Fawcett when he heard what he said about him in his final speech.

A few days before the case came on, a consultation was held by the defendants' committee with both Fawcett and Hall. Fawcett's consultations were always conducted at a leisurely pace. Although he was overwhelmed with work, he was like a good general medical practitioner who gives the impression that yours is his only case.

'How's our witness?' Fawcett asked.

'Very well, Sir Maxwell,' said Springfold. 'I have, of course, assumed that this is not one of those rare cases in which you'd like to see her yourself.'

'Good gracious no,' said Fawcett. 'You agree, Hall, I suppose?'

Enton Hall was not in any sense a yes-man. If he disagreed with his learned leader he said so in no uncertain terms, though in a somewhat hesitant manner which at first deceived those, who did not know him, into thinking he was in some doubt. But on this occasion he was of the same view as Fawcett.

'Entirely,' he said.

'Well, I'm glad she's in good heart. Have your clients insured her life, by the way? Although her written statements might be admissible, they wouldn't make the same impression as her sworn evidence.'

'Yes,' said Springfold. 'That's been taken care of.'

'Good,' said Fawcett. 'She's a very valuable young woman at the moment. Does she realise it?'

'Well, she couldn't avoid realising it,' said Springfold. 'We're treating her more carefully than Royalty. But she hasn't attempted to take advantage of the fact. Her only worry is the possibility of her husband finding out. But I really do think we've got that tied up as far as is humanly possible, provided the judge plays. And you're sure he will, aren't you, Sir Maxwell?'

'As sure as one can be of anything. And, of course, sorry as I should be for Mrs Verney if anything were disclosed, by that time she'd have given her evidence, and that's all that's necessary from the defendants' point of view. It's a pity you can't find out anything to Sampson's discredit, but from what you tell me of Mrs Verney she's more likely to get the sympathy of the jury than the plaintiff.'

'I shall be surprised if she doesn't,' said Springfold.

'What arrangements have you made for her coming to Court?'

'Well, she'll come straight to my office after her husband goes out, and stay there until she's either wanted as a witness or the Court adjourns. I can guarantee her arrival in Court at any time on five minutes' notice.'

'Now, one of the things I want to discuss is this,' said Fawcett. 'We admit publication and the onus of proving justification is upon us. Shall we claim the right to begin? Or shall we see what attitude the other side takes? In some ways I'd like to get Mrs Verney through the box first. It must be a trying time for her and the less waiting she has, the better. On the other hand, if she gives evidence after Sampson, they retire with her version the last given. What d'you think, Enton?'

'I think wait and see. It might be that he'd like us to accept the burden but doesn't like to say so in front of the jury. In that case we play into his hands by offering to accept it. If he asks us to begin, the jury may think he's frightened to go into the witness box and, even if he subsequently does give evidence, there's a bit against him in their eyes from the beginning. No, I think let him begin or make him ask us to. In any event in view of the libels we are not justifying, he has the right to begin if he wants to.'

'Well,' said Fawcett, 'what's your view, Mr Springfold?'

'I'm very happy to leave it to you and Mr Hall. I'm sure that whatever you agree upon will be the right course.'

'That doesn't follow,' said Fawcett, 'but I'm glad to say that Mr Hall is not one of those counsel who make me think I must be wrong if they agree with me. I think you're right, Enton. We'll wait and see. And that leads me to another matter. Edward Verney. We've promised not to get in touch with him. Either Sampson will call him or he won't. If he does call him to corroborate his story, I think we'll be in a mess, because that will really show that Mrs

Verney's story's untrue. Though personally I cannot conceive why she should invent it. However, we'll be shown to be wrong if Mr Verney is called. But conversely, if he isn't called, that puts Sampson in an almost impossible position. One advantage of letting the plaintiff open is that we'll know whether Verney is being called. If he isn't, it seems to me we'll have won even before we've called his wife. I can't think of any legitimate excuse for Sampson's not calling him. If Verney really employed him, can you see how he can win without calling him, Enton?'

'He could call him and lose,' said Hall. 'Out of revenge, I mean. That would make our clients look pretty silly with all their promises to Mrs Verney. She's been told she's quite safe if she's telling the truth. But she isn't, you know. For example, Sampson could just have him in Court without calling him.'

'But is he likely to do that?' asked Fawcett. 'It'd make his prosecution almost certain. It's obvious that the Director's waiting to see what happens. If Sampson loses and his story about being employed by Verney is shown to be untrue, at the very least there's a reasonable chance of his conviction, isn't there? He doesn't *want* to go to prison does he? It's not worth venting one's spite if it involves years in jail. No, if Verney is brought to Court by Sampson, it'll be because his story is true. In that case Mrs Verney comes to no harm because it means that her husband in fact knew all about her. Moreover it serves her right for telling lies. 'Whatever happens, I don't think our clients can have anything to reproach themselves with. They undertook not to interview Verney and they haven't. Incidentally, they haven't in the least hurt themselves by not doing so. It's true that in a prosecution it would be up to the Crown to call him. But in the civil proceedings there is every reason why the defendants are entitled to leave it to the plaintiff to call him, and to comment very strongly indeed if he doesn't. In my view if he calls him we're sunk, and, if he doesn't, he is. I don't think there's any half way house. And I think that Mrs Verney, as a married woman who went to an hotel with another man and has never confessed to her husband, will not be able to complain of her treatment.'

CHAPTER TWENTY-FIVE

Counsel's Opinion

It was only natural that the question of calling Mr Verney to give evidence was also a subject of conversation between Mr Sampson and his advisers.

'Of course he'll corroborate what I say,' said Mr Sampson at his conference with his counsel, Mr Felsham.

'I know you say that, but, if you're so sure, why don't you let Mr Seaworthy get a statement from him?'

'Because he hates solicitors and interviews. He doesn't like coming to Court, but he'll come. He's promised.'

'But it would be much better if we had him subpoenaed. Then he'd have to come.'

'Would it?' said Mr Sampson. 'He might go abroad or, worse, tell lies about me?'

'That would be perjury,' said Mr Felsham.

'And who's to prove it, except me?' asked Mr Sampson. 'Even if he could be convicted that wouldn't be much use to me if I'd lost the case. But anyway you need two witnesses to convict of perjury, don't you?'

'That's true,' said Mr Felsham, 'but I must say I don't like this uncertainty. At least you might have let him be interviewed. I hate calling people blind.'

'Meaning?' asked Mr Sampson.

'Calling a witness when I haven't a statement from him. How am I to know what he's going to say?'

'I've told you.'

'That's second-hand. I like it first-hand. All the same, it's your case and if, after your solicitor's very strong warning that he ought at least to be interviewed, if not subpoenaed, you decide to reject that advice, then you won't be able to complain if he lets you down.'

'Right,' said Mr Sampson. 'Now, let me put this to you. I'm the one who knows Verney, aren't I?'

'So you say,' said Mr Felsham. 'We've only your word for the fact that you've even spoken to the man.'

'Right. So you have. Now I tell you that this particular witness is a very touchy person, that he doesn't like you gentlemen, that he hates Courts and such like, and that he says he'll only come to Court to help me if we don't worry him beforehand. Now, Mr Felsham, you're my counsel, will you take the risk of saying that he *is* to be interviewed or is to be subpoenaed? He's the only independent witness, isn't he? If he supports my case, we're home, aren't we? If he puts a spanner in the works what happens then? It's quite true that people are supposed to tell the truth in the witness box, but they don't always, do they? There are no documents. So he's only got to say he never employed me and where are we? Now you've tried to throw the blame on me, Mr Felsham, if things go wrong. I beg to return the compliment. It's going to be your fault in any event, Mr Felsham.'

'Why?' asked Mr Felsham a little petulantly.

'Because you're going to make the choice, if you please. Which is it to be? Statement and subpoena? Or neither, and rely on me to get him there? Well, Mr Felsham, it's up to you. You're in command. But I'll only add this. Have I been proved wrong yet in anything I've said to you? Look at all the hullabaloo they made out about me in the papers. If half of it were true, I'd be in prison for life. But nothing's happened. No arrest. No prosecution. It's I who've taken action, Mr Felsham, not the police. And when they put in their defence, what does it all come to? One charge only, and the only corroboration on our side – that's Mr Verney. Well, how's he going to come to Court, Mr Felsham? Under his own steam or handcuffed to my solicitor?'

'Well, Mr Sampson, I think you're pretty offensive, but that doesn't mean you're wrong. You are the person who knows the witness best, and I shall have to rely on you. Basing my opinion on what you tell me – basing my opinion *entirely* on what you tell me – so that the responsibility will be yours, Mr Sampson, if what you tell me is not correct, on that basis and in spite of my instincts to the contrary, Mr Verney shall be left to come to Court under his own steam and without a previous interview. But you will make sure he's there at the right time, won't you?'

'I will do my best,' said Mr Sampson. 'As you advise that he should not be subpoenaed that's all I can do. My best. But that's been quite good so far.'

CHAPTER TWENTY-SIX

Mr Sampson's Trial

The case started on a Monday before Mr Justice Mellow and a jury, and the Court was crowded when Mr Felsham rose to open for the plaintiff. What was he going to do? Was he going to open or throw the burden on the defendants? If he opened, was he going to call Verney? The defendants soon learned the answer to the first question.

After he had formally announced the names of the parties and of counsel appearing for them he went on: 'This is a libel action, members of the jury, or rather it is a series of actions which all parties have agreed shall be tried together, but if you come to a conclusion in favour of the plaintiff you will have to award separate damages against each of the defendants. Now libel, subject to anything his Lordship may tell you, consists in this Court of a false statement in writing injurious to a man's character. I venture to think you will have no difficulty in coming to a conclusion on the first matter which you have to decide. The defendants admit publication of the various headlines and paragraphs complained of. Were they calculated to injure the plaintiff's character? The answer to that question is simple enough. The plaintiff was called a blackmailer. Could a more damaging statement be made about a man? Well – yes it could. He could have been called a murderer as well. He could have been called a lot of other things, but you may think that blackmailer is almost as bad an allegation to make against a man as you can think of, unless it is true. And that, members of the jury, is really the whole issue in this case. Is my client a blackmailer? The defendants have the boldness to say that in substance what they published was true and that they will prove it.

'Members of the jury, it is for them to prove it, and I could, had I chosen, have kept the plaintiff out of the witness box and called on the defendants to prove their case. For his Lordship will tell you, I think, that it is not for my client to prove his innocence but for the newspapers to prove his guilt. However, I feel sure that you would prefer to see in the witness box as soon as possible the man against whom these dreadful allegations were made, and see what sort of a man he is. He is hiding behind no technical pleas of who has to prove what. I shall call him before you as my first witness.

'Now, before I open the facts of the case to you, members of the jury, it is right that I should tell you this. In some of the publications complained of all kinds of allegations are made against the plaintiff. It is even suggested that he has pursued a systematic course of blackmailing members of my profession throughout the Temple and Lincoln's Inn. The defendants do not seek to justify any of these allegations. They say, and say only, that he blackmailed a lady who, with his Lordship's permission, I shall call Mrs X. That is the only truth they say there is in these wholesale allegations. There is no defence to what I may call the extra allegations. It would not even be necessary for my client to give evidence if he did not wish to do so. The only question here is what are the damages.

'In spite of that, members of the jury, if you were in fact satisfied that my client had blackmailed Mrs X, I should not take up much of your time in asking you for damages for the other statements. Blackmail is such an appalling crime that, if you were satisfied that the case was proved in one instance, I concede at once that the fact that other false allegations of the same kind were made, wrong though it was to make them, wrong though it was to allow such influential newspapers to be influenced by a kind of hysteria that seemed to sweep through EC4, wrong though these things were, I nevertheless should not suggest that any substantial sum should be paid for saying them about a man who in your opinion had blackmailed Mrs X. But if, members of the jury, you are satisfied that he did nothing of the kind, then you may think that the damages should be very large indeed, and, just as I have not asked for any substantial damages if you convict my client of blackmailing Mrs X, so I expect my learned opponent not to resist the payment of very heavy damages indeed if you decide that matter in my client's favour.

'So the first question you will have to decide is – was Mrs X blackmailed by my client. Now the facts in relation to my client's association with Mrs X are as follows.'

Mr Felsham then outlined the facts as he was instructed by Mr Sampson. He said nothing about calling Verney before he said: 'I will now call the evidence. Mr Sampson, will you kindly go into the witness box.'

Fawcett turned to his junior and whispered: 'They can't be calling Verney or he'd have said so.'

But the fact was that Felsham, being of a cautious nature, was not going to say anything about Verney until he actually had him in the witness box. If the man duly appeared, his evidence would be more effective rather than less by reason of its not being mentioned before. If he never appeared, at any rate he would not have opened the case on the basis that he was going to give evidence.

Mr Sampson gave his evidence quite well when examined by Mr Felsham, and then Fawcett rose to cross-examine. He questioned him about the interviews with Margaret, and put Margaret's story to him. Mr Sampson denied that he had ever suggested she should pay him money and he repeated that he had been employed by Mr X to make enquiries about Mrs X. Fawcett reserved what he thought would be his best point until his final question.

'And are we going to have the privilege of seeing Mr X in the witness box?'

'Certainly,' said Mr Sampson. 'He's sitting down there,' and he pointed to Edward Verney who was sitting in the back of the court.

This was a very nasty jolt for Fawcett and his clients. If Edward were going to confirm Mr Sampson's story, and if he stood up to cross-examination, things would look very black indeed for the defendants. And, apart from that, there was the fact that it would be necessary to tell Margaret at some time that her husband was going to be in Court. She might refuse to come, and, though she could be made to do so, in her anxiety or anger she might say anything in the witness box. When the case was adjourned for the day, Fawcett told Springfold not to tell Margaret about her husband's presence until the last moment.

'I'll take the responsibility. She has said that Sampson would never get him there. If her story's untrue and Sampson's is true, she deserves what she gets for misleading us. In that case I suppose Verney has said nothing about it to her so far because he wants to get her sworn admission about the Fisherman's Nook. Hasn't got sufficient evidence otherwise, or something.'

'In spite of everything,' said Springfold, 'I cannot see why she should be lying. What has she got to gain from it? It seems a pretty cumbersome way of trying to discredit an enquiry agent.'

At the adjournment Fawcett and Felsham left the Court together. They chatted on the way.

'You didn't seem to care for my client's last answer,' said Felsham.

'I did not,' said Fawcett.

'Want to make me an offer?'

'Not yet, thank you. As our old friend Grimes would have said, "we shall see, my dear fellow, we shall see." '

'We shall,' said Felsham confidently. Previously he had told Mr Sampson to see that Verney was at the Court punctually at 10.30 next morning.

Margaret had spent the whole of the day in her solicitor's office from 10.30 onwards. She was told that 11 a.m. would be early enough for the next day.

The following morning she duly arrived at 11 o'clock and was told that the case had been adjourned to the next day. What had happened was this. As soon as the case was called on Felsham had said: 'I'll call Mr X. Mr X, will you kindly go into the witness box?'

Nothing happened. Mr Felsham glanced behind him, and, as he did not see the witness in Court, said: 'May the witness be called outside Court, my Lord?' The usher went outside and could be heard calling – 'Mr X – Mr X …'

'He may not realise who that is,' said the judge. 'Let your client go out and find him.'

So Mr Sampson and his solicitor went outside the Court but there was no sign of Verney. They brought the bad news to Felsham.

'Are you sure you told him to be here at 10.30?' Felsham asked Mr Sampson in an undertone.

'Yes, and he promised he would be.'

'There's nothing like a subpoena, is there?' said Felsham grimly.

'If he's been knocked down by a bus,' said Mr Sampson, 'a subpoena wouldn't bring him to.'

'My Lord,' said Felsham, 'I find myself in a difficulty. The witness is not present, and at the moment I can give no reason for his absence. He may have had an accident. I can only ask your Lordship for the indulgence of a short adjournment so that further enquiries can be made.'

'Very well,' said the judge. 'Has the witness been subpoenaed?'

'No, my Lord,' said Mr Felsham.

'Then he should have been,' said the judge.

Mr Felsham turned and looked at his client, who whispered: 'The judge doesn't know everything.'

As soon as the judge rose, Mr Sampson said that he would make immediate enquiries. He came back to the court an hour later and said that he had had no luck. The only person he could ask about his movements was Mrs Verney and that, in the circumstances, did not seem possible. The judge was brought back into Court, and Felsham successfully applied for an adjournment to the next day. After all, it was possible that there *had* been an accident.

'I'm sorry, members of the jury,' said the judge. 'It is inconvenient for everyone but it would not be fair to the plaintiff not to give him an opportunity to see what has happened to Mr X. In the present notorious state of the roads an accident is not an absurd suggestion. Or the man may have been taken ill. But, Mr Felsham, if the witness is alive and well he must be in that witness box at half past ten tomorrow morning. If your clients have chosen not to subpoena him, that is their responsibility. I shall not grant a further adjournment except for very good cause.'

At 10.15 next morning, neither Mr Sampson nor Verney had arrived at Court and both Felsham and his professional client were getting anxious. But at 10.30 Mr Sampson rushed in excitedly.

'Look what I've just had,' he said.

It was a note from Edward Verney.

Dear Mr Sampson,

I am so sorry that, after all, I shall not be able to help you at your trial. I have been called abroad suddenly. I am so sorry and hope it won't inconvenience you too much. Thank you so much for your help.

Yours sincerely,

Edward Verney.

'Now, there's no point in saying you warned me,' Mr Sampson said to Felsham. 'What happens now?'

'You probably lose the case,' said Felsham.

He showed the note to Fawcett.

'I suppose you won't let me put it in?' he asked his opponent, though not very hopefully.

'You suppose right,' said Fawcett cheerfully. 'Want to make me an offer?'

The situation had turned remarkably in the defendants' favour and there was a very happy look on the faces of the Committee and all their legal representatives as the judge came in.

'Get Mrs Verney here at once,' said Fawcett to Springfold. 'I'll be about twenty minutes or so in opening. So you've lots of time.'

The case was called and Felsham rose and explained to the judge that unfortunately he would not be in a position to call the witness.

'Any explanation?' asked the judge.

'There is one but my learned friend is not prepared for me to give it.'

'Very well, then. Call your next witness, please.'

'That is the plaintiff's case.'

'Yes, Sir Maxwell?' said the judge, inviting him to open the defendants' case.

'May it please your Lordship,' he said. 'Members of the jury, my learned opponent and I may disagree on several topics during this case, but there is one on which we are plainly agreed. Blackmail is a terrible crime. Another thing we shall agree upon. It is a very grave thing to call a man a blackmailer. Whether we shall agree that it is normally difficult to prove that a man is a blackmailer I do not know, but I accept that it is. Nevertheless, that is what the defendants have undertaken to do, and when the whole of the evidence has been heard, members of the jury, I shall ask you to say that they have made good their undertaking. Cases are, of course, decided upon the evidence, members of the jury, but in considering the evidence that *has* been called, you are also entitled to consider that which has *not* been called but which you might have expected to have been called.

'Mr Sampson has sworn that he was employed by Mr X to make enquiries about Mrs X and that was the reason for his visits to her. Once again I think my learned friend would agree with me – however discomforting the reflection in the circumstances – I think he would be forced to agree that the obvious witness for Mr Sampson to call to support his case would be Mr X. Indeed we have Mr Sampson's word for it that Mr X was in Court. Only his word, mark you. But when Mr X was called to give evidence yesterday he did not appear and, in spite of my Lord's indulgence, he did not appear today either.

'Now my learned friend showed me a piece of paper said to contain the explanation for Mr X's absence. Now, members of the jury, if that piece of paper had been a doctor's certificate or a note from a hospital or police station or something of that kind to account for Mr X's absence, I should, of course, have allowed it to have been put before you. It is no technical objection I am taking to the supposed explanation for Mr X's absence. We do not in fact know for certain that it was Mr X who was here on Monday. We only have Mr Sampson's word for it. The piece of paper I was handed was in a handwriting none of us know – and I doubt if my learned friend knows it either – it was a document which might or might not be an authentic document at all. If Mr Sampson has done what I hope to prove that he has done, he would be perfectly capable of procuring such a document to be made in the hope that it might explain away or help to excuse the absence of this important – you may think vital – witness.

'Now, members of the jury, if my learned friend had said to me – indeed if he says to me now that I can have his word for it that Mr X was in Court on Monday and that he can vouch for the authenticity of the document he showed me, then, members of the jury, I shall at once withdraw my objection to your seeing it and it can be produced in evidence. I pause for a moment to see if the very reasonable assurances for which I ask are forthcoming. My learned friend says nothing. Is it a wry smile I detect on his face? No matter. He says nothing. He does not vouch for the authenticity of the document. He does not even vouch for the fact that Mr X was here on Monday.

'You may think that it would not be beyond the wit of a blackmailer – and that it requires nerve and imagination to be one you may have no doubt – it would not be beyond the wit of a blackmailer, who knew that he could not call this vital witness, to have someone in Court one day whom he pretends to be the witness, and then to produce an unauthenticated document the next day to try to account for his absence. Members of the jury, I venture to suggest to you that Mr Sampson knew he could never call Mr X. Why was he not subpoenaed? That wouldn't have done, would it, members of the jury, because either the real Mr X would have arrived – and that you may imagine would not have suited the plaintiff at all – or an impersonator would have arrived and that wouldn't have suited either Mr Sampson or the impersonator at all. It's one thing just to be pointed to in Court, quite another thing to go up into the hbhbhg and swear you are someone whom you are not. Mr Sampson's confederate – as you may well think he was – was prepared to sit in Court and allow himself to be pointed at. That was no offence. But perjury is still an offence, members of the jury, although perhaps the ratio of prosecutions to offences is minute.

'Nevertheless, in this case a man might well have hesitated to describe himself as someone he was not, living at a place where he did not live, doing a job which he did not do. It would not have taken a great deal of effort to prove the perjury in such a case, and the impersonator may well have thought that prosecution would almost inevitably follow. So I hope, members of the jury, you will not think I am putting the case too high when I suggest that the plaintiff did not call Mr X because he knew that he could not do so.

'Having said that, members of the jury, I am quite content if you forget what happened on Monday and a few minutes ago. As far as I am concerned, you may treat the case just as though none of that happened and that the plaintiff simply closed his case without calling Mr X.

'That indeed, members of the jury, is what has happened. Here is a man who could have corroborated up to the hilt the plaintiff's reason for visiting Mrs X. It is conceded by implication that he is alive and well. But the plaintiff does not call him. This plaintiff who complains of being called a blackmailer, who through his eloquent and learned counsel has pointed out that the publicity has ruined him, that this case is life and death to him and that nothing but enormous damages can make up to him for the damage inflicted on him by the defendants, this plaintiff, without the slightest explanation, simply does not call the man.

'You may wonder why he brought the case, members of the jury, if he were not in a position to call Mr X. Why should a man in his position challenge the entire newspaper world of the country if he knows he hasn't the evidence to win his case? I dare say you may have thought of the answer yourselves. Do you think perhaps that the plaintiff was trying to put off the evil day when his crime – I repeat, his crime – would be dealt with in the Court where it belongs? Do you think that he may have been trying to snatch a few more months of liberty before he is rightly and properly deprived of that liberty for a considerable period?

'Members of the jury, so far I have addressed you on the defendant's lack of evidence, and I venture to suggest that his own case as it stands is a miserable, tottering affair which it would not take much to push over, if, indeed, it is still standing. As my learned friend remains in his place and does not offer to consent to judgment against his client, I must assume that he is going on with this withered effigy of a case. Well, then, let me tell you that defendants, such as those for whom I appear, would not justify such a grave allegation as the one in this case unless they had evidence, and strong evidence, to support their plea. Not a phantom witness such as the one we have just heard about but a real live person who, desperately anxious though she is that her husband shall not hear her evidence, is coming to this Court to tell you what happened when she let the plaintiff into her flat, and was compelled by fear to let him in again and yet again.

'Members of the jury, I do not mind telling you that both I and my clients were seriously worried when the plaintiff in the witness box pointed, as he said, to Mr X in Court. It would have been, for reasons which you shall hear, a terrible ordeal for Mrs X to have to give her evidence in the presence of her husband. For no doubt you realise that the witness I am referring to is Mrs X. I must also admit that the very presence of Mr X in Court cast in my mind some doubt about the truth of the story which Mrs X is to tell you. Lesser people than the defendants might have given in at that stage. But fortunately my clients have a deep sense of responsibility and they were not content to accept the mere word of the plaintiff that Mr X was to be called. Truth, members of the jury, it has been said, has a nasty habit of coming out. And you may well think, when you have heard Mrs X's evidence, not only that truth shines throughout her story but that it is fully corroborated by the miserable performance which you have just witnessed, in what you may think is a desperate attempt by the plaintiff to delay the just retribution that is slowly but surely advancing towards him.

'I am not going to detain you further, members of the jury. I shall let Mrs X tell her own story. It will come better from her than from me. We are only mouthpieces, nothing that we say is evidence. What you require is the sworn testimony, not of someone who is here today and gone tomorrow, but of someone who is here today *and* tomorrow and tomorrow's morrow if need be. Call Mrs X.'

Felsham had listened to Fawcett's oratory unhappily. Although counsel should not identify himself with his client, while the fight is on he often feels the punches as much as his client, indeed sometimes more so, as he better realises their object and effect. Several times during Fawcett's opening, Felsham had been tempted to get up and protest against the play which was being made by his opponent with a document which had not been put in evidence and which the jury could not see. Fawcett had indeed pretty successfully induced the idea that the document was a forgery without Felsham's client being given a chance to deal with the allegation. Two things prevented him from intervening. In the first place he himself had said that Fawcett would not allow him to give the explanation for Mr X's absence. If he intervened he could hear his opponent say something like: 'I am not surprised my learned friend is a little anxious about the matter. You may think that anyone would be in his position. But he must be pretty far gone to try to prevent me from defending myself from an allegation he himself made. He said that I would not allow the explanation for Mr X's absence to be made. Perhaps he regrets having said that, but, as he has said it, am I not to be allowed to explain why I would not allow it?'

The judge would probably say that Fawcett was justified in giving his explanation, and he would have done more harm than good by his intervention. That was the second reason for his silence. To intervene would be to disclose to the jury that the blows were going home, and that could only make them pay even more attention to them. Later on, if necessary, he could ask for leave to recall his client to deal with the allegations. Meanwhile he sat silent trying to look, as every good advocate in an awkward position tries to do, completely unconcerned with what his opponent was saying. Advocates vary in their ability to preserve a mask of indifference. It would be improper to make faces at the jury, or to do anything to take the jury's mind off the points being made by the other side. On the other hand, no one can complain that an advocate remains completely still and unmoved. Yet there is a way of doing this which suggests: 'What is this fellow belly-aching about? How long is he going to trouble us with his blusterings? What a lot of nonsense it all is, isn't it? But I'm sure an intelligent judge and an intelligent jury can see through it!' It was this sort of impassivity that Felsham tried to reproduce and on the whole it was a pretty impressive performance. On the other hand, the strength of Fawcett's attack and the logic behind it were such that it required more than the most brilliant feat of silence on the part of Mr Sampson's counsel to counteract the effect of the speech.

While nevertheless preserving his expression of nonchalance, Felsham was also cursing his client for not allowing a subpoena. He did not believe for a moment the suggestion that Mr X had not been in Court the day before and, if only he had been served with a subpoena, he'd have been bound to attend Court. Moreover, the note itself showed two things, one that Mr X knew Mr Sampson, and secondly that Mr Sampson had done something for Mr X for which the latter thanked him. All entirely consistent with his client's story.

Barristers naturally like to win their cases, but if, without any mistake made by anyone, they lose them, they accept defeat philosophically. But to lose a case which could have been won through one's advice being disregarded was most frustrating. That it was the client's fault was little consolation. His only chance now was if he could break up Mrs X in cross-examination, but he very much doubted if he could do this. He had very little material with which to do so, and he would have to be very careful in cross-examining a woman who, according to his information, was charming and attractive in appearance, lest he alienated the jury. However, he must do his best with the lady, and he waited patiently for her to go into the witness box.

He tried to think of some unusual question with which he might start his cross-examination and which might baffle the witness and interest the jury. It was only when he realised that he had been doing this for what seemed quite a time that he glanced towards his opponent, ready to meet the flushed face of prospective success with his mask of disinterest when, to his surprise, he saw that Fawcett's face was indeed flushed but not with the prospects of success. Excited whispers were going on between him and his solicitor. Soon the judge wanted to know what was happening.

'Come along,' he said, 'let's get on. 'Where is Mrs X?'

That indeed was the question. Instead of bringing the witness to Court an excited young solicitor had brought a note to Mr Springfold. It was from Mrs X.

I am dreadfully sorry about this, *she wrote*, but something wonderful has just happened. My husband suddenly said that, if I'd go away with him at once, he'd try to forget the other woman. He'd had a row with her, and I felt sure that if I didn't seize the chance at once with both hands they might make it up. I think that he realised this too, and wanted the excuse to get back to me but was frightened of himself, was afraid that he couldn't resist her if she came back to him. I'm sure that's why he booked an air passage at once and wanted me to come immediately. I just had to go. I am so very sorry, but I'm sure you realise that for me it is my whole life, while yours is only a case. You have treated me so well during these anxious months that I hope you will believe how sorry I am to let you down, but if you are a married man and in love with your wife I hope you will understand. By the time you get this I shall be in the air. I am already treading on it.

With so many regrets and thanks,

Margaret Verney.

'Would your Lordship give me a moment or two?' asked Fawcett.

'Yes,' said the judge, but added testily: 'We've already wasted a good deal of time over a missing witness. Be as quick as you can, please.'

There were more murmurings and whisperings on the defendants' side of the court.

'My Lord,' said Fawcett, after about a minute, 'I am extremely sorry to inconvenience your Lordship and the jury, but, just as my learned friend craved your indulgence the day before yesterday, may I do so now?'

'How long d'you want?' asked the judge.

'Could your Lordship rise for ten minutes?'

'Very well, then. Ten minutes, but no more.'

The judge rose and Fawcett went across to Felsham.

'Here is my *billet doux*,' he said.

Felsham read it.

'It looks as though you did my man an injustice. The X's have gone off together. What are you going to do about it?'

'I shall ask for an adjournment.'

'How long for?'

'Till we can find out where the birds have flown.'

'How d'you know they'll come back?'

'Well, we could ask for her evidence to be taken on commission abroad.'

'Only if she's willing. You can't force her to give evidence unless she's in this country.'

'Well I shall apply anyway.'

The judge was asked to come back into Court.

'This is most unsatisfactory and inconvenient,' he said, when Fawcett made his application, 'but I don't see how justice can properly be done unless I give you a little time to find out what the witness' intentions are and whether her evidence can be taken abroad.'

The case was accordingly adjourned and the defendants managed to get in touch with Margaret at an hotel in Madeira. Mr Springfold spoke to her on the telephone.

'I doubt if we'll ever come back to England,' she said. 'We are blissfully happy and England has unhappy associations for us. No, I'm afraid I don't want to have anything more to do with the case. No, I'm so sorry. That's final. I do apologise.'

The day after the telephone conversation Fawcett asked Felsham to call on him.

'You've got us,' he said. 'We can't go on without Mrs X. So it's only a question of damages. How much d'you want? My clients will be generous. They'll have to be. What about £10,000 altogether?'

'You're not being serious?' said Felsham. 'You call a man a blackmailer, justify, cross-examine him as though he

were one, and then make a speech that must be worth
more than £10,000 by itself. No, my boy,' said Felsham,
'there's no point in discussing the matter if that's what you
call your clients' generosity. I'm quite prepared to take one
lump sum and I don't mind how you split it up among
your clients, but it must be six figures or we'll fight.
Whatever you pay into Court at this late stage and
whatever we recover, we'll get the bulk of the costs. So
you'll have to pay in a lot to tempt me.'

'If your client wants £100,000 or more you must ask the
jury for them.'

'I hoped you'd say that,' said Felsham. 'I want to remind
the jury of some of the things you said about him.'

So the case came on again and Fawcett announced that
the defendants would no longer persist in their defence
and would only contest the claim for damages.

'Before I make my closing speech,' said Felsham, 'might
I know if the defendants are offering any apologies to my
client? Are they unreservedly withdrawing all the
allegations?'

'By saying that the defence is no longer persisted in we
automatically withdraw the charges,' said Fawcett. His
clients were very angry. They knew they would have to pay
a large sum anyway and they were in no mood to
apologise, even though the lack of it might increase the
damages still more.

'A most gracious way of doing it,' commented Felsham.
He then proceeded to make a most telling speech to the
jury, calling attention to the vast publicity accorded to the
charges, to the defendants' persistence in them right up to
the last moment, to Fawcett's opening speech, and to the
failure to apologise.

'The defendants say that they have had to abandon their defence because they cannot call their only witness. They too received a little note. I hope you will bear in mind that I am not suggesting that that note is a forgery. Although I am not prepared to allow the contents to be revealed, without the opportunity of cross-examining the lady who wrote it, I am quite satisfied that she did write it, and I should have thought that by now the defendants would have been satisfied that the note which I showed to my learned friend was equally genuine. But, whatever they may now think, not a word of apology is forthcoming. Subject to anything his Lordship may say to you, I submit to you, members of the jury, that the whole of the conduct of the defendants may be taken into consideration when you are assessing the damages in these cases, and I must confess that I think I should find it difficult to exaggerate the kind of award to which my client is entitled.'

By this time Fawcett, far from looking as Felsham had done during *his* opening speech, was shifting uncomfortably in his seat and exchanging notes with his solicitor. Eventually he passed a note to Felsham while he was still speaking. It simply had '£100,000' on it.

'Done,' said Felsham quickly. He had already had instructions from his client to accept such an offer. The judge was informed that the Court and jury would no longer be troubled with the case, and judgment was entered for Mr Sampson for £100,000 and costs.

'Well, Mr Seaworthy tells me they had served a subpoena,' said Mr Sampson to Felsham, after he had thanked him, 'but it didn't seem to help them!'

A few weeks later Mr Sampson paid £100,000 into his bank and reviewed the operation. He doubted if it would be necessary for him to indulge in any similar operations, but it was as well to learn from one's mistakes. Had he made any? On careful consideration he thought not. When he had first learned from an acquaintance of Moriarty about Culsworth's misbehaviour, he and his friends the Verneys had wondered how the information could be converted into cash. Blackmail was much too dangerous a game and was even distasteful to people of feeling like Mr Sampson and Mr and Mrs Verney. But huge damages for libel obtained from newspapers could be enjoyed without any twinge of conscience. After all, if newspapers will refer to incidents as 'murder' or 'blackmail' before anyone has been convicted of the crime, they must expect to have to pay up from time to time.

If the information about Culsworth turned out to be false they would have lost nothing except time. If it were true, the moment to begin was when he appeared in some big or unusual case. His withdrawal from the Baker case seemed a most opportune moment to start. With blackmail apparently going on in the fiat above his chambers he was almost bound to think that it would be his turn next. After that it was easy to convey the impression that the occupants of the Temple were being generally victimised.

So, having concocted their plan, Margaret and he had played their parts as though they were complete strangers, so that her story about the interviews should sound true. She had to live the part in order to be really convincing. When Mr Springfold and Culsworth felt sure that she was telling them something that had really happened they were in a sense perfectly right.

After that everything went perfectly. No, he could not fault himself anywhere. But good Heavens! he suddenly thought, how disgraceful of me! He at once obtained a banker's draft for £50,000 and sent it to Mr & Mrs Basil Merridew (the name to which the Verneys had reverted after leaving Madeira). After all, most of the credit was due to Basil, whose idea it was. Mr Sampson had only been an actor. The author and director was fully entitled to his share, even if he only came on to the stage once.

HENRY CECIL

ACCORDING TO THE EVIDENCE

Alec Morland is on trial for murder. He has tried to remedy the ineffectiveness of the law by taking matters into his own hands. Unfortunately for him, his alleged crime was not committed in immediate defence of others or of himself. In this fascinating murder trial you will not find out until the very end just how the law will interpret his actions. Will his defence be accepted or does a different fate await him?

THE ASKING PRICE

Ronald Holbrook is a fifty-seven-year-old bachelor who has lived in the same house for twenty years. Jane Doughty, the daughter of his next-door neighbours, is seventeen. She suddenly decides she is in love with Ronald and wants to marry him. Everyone is amused at first but then events take a disturbingly sinister turn and Ronald finds himself enmeshed in a potentially tragic situation.

'The secret of Mr Cecil's success lies in continuing to do superbly what everyone now knows he can do well.'
The Sunday Times

HENRY CECIL

BRIEF TALES FROM THE BENCH

What does it feel like to be a Judge? Read these stories and you can almost feel you are looking at proceedings from the lofty position of the Bench.

With a collection of eccentric and amusing characters, Henry Cecil brings to life the trials in a County Court and exposes the complex and often contradictory workings of the English legal system.

'Immensely readable. His stories rely above all on one quality – an extraordinary, an arresting, a really staggering ingenuity.'
New Statesman

BROTHERS IN LAW

Roger Thursby, aged twenty-four, is called to the bar. He is young, inexperienced and his love life is complicated. He blunders his way through a succession of comic adventures including his calamitous debut at the bar.

His career takes an upward turn when he is chosen to defend the caddish Alfred Green at the Old Bailey. In this first Roger Thursby novel Henry Cecil satirizes the legal profession with his usual wit and insight.

'Uproariously funny.' *The Times*

'Full of charm and humour. I think it is the best Henry Cecil yet.' P G Wodehouse

Henry Cecil

Hunt the Slipper

Harriet and Graham have been happily married for twenty years. One day Graham fails to return home and Harriet begins to realise she has been abandoned. This feeling is strengthened when she starts to receive monthly payments from an untraceable source. After five years on her own Harriet begins to see another man and divorces Graham on the grounds of his desertion. Then one evening Harriet returns home to find Graham sitting in a chair, casually reading a book. Her initial relief turns to anger and then to fear when she realises that if Graham's story is true, she may never trust his sanity again. This complex comedy thriller will grip your attention to the very last page.

Sober as a Judge

Roger Thursby, the hero of *Brothers in Law* and *Friends at Court*, continues his career as a High Court judge. He presides over a series of unusual cases, including a professional debtor and an action about a consignment of oranges which turned to juice before delivery. There is a delightful succession of eccentric witnesses as the reader views proceedings from the Bench.

'The author's gift for brilliant characterisation makes this a book that will delight lawyers and laymen as much as did its predecessors.' *The Daily Telegraph*

OTHER TITLES BY HENRY CECIL AVAILABLE DIRECT
FROM HOUSE OF STRATUS

Quantity		£	$(US)	$(CAN)	€
	ACCORDING TO THE EVIDENCE	6.99	11.50	15.99	11.50
	ALIBI FOR A JUDGE	6.99	11.50	15.99	11.50
	THE ASKING PRICE	6.99	11.50	15.99	11.50
	BRIEF TALES FROM THE BENCH	6.99	11.50	15.99	11.50
	BROTHERS IN LAW	6.99	11.50	15.99	11.50
	THE BUTTERCUP SPELL	6.99	11.50	15.99	11.50
	CROSS PURPOSES	6.99	11.50	15.99	11.50
	DAUGHTERS IN LAW	6.99	11.50	15.99	11.50
	FATHERS IN LAW	6.99	11.50	15.99	11.50
	FRIENDS AT COURT	6.99	11.50	15.99	11.50
	FULL CIRCLE	6.99	11.50	15.99	11.50
	HUNT THE SLIPPER	6.99	11.50	15.99	11.50
	INDEPENDENT WITNESS	6.99	11.50	15.99	11.50

ALL HOUSE OF STRATUS BOOKS ARE AVAILABLE FROM GOOD BOOKSHOPS OR
DIRECT FROM THE PUBLISHER:

Internet: **www.houseofstratus.com** including author interviews, reviews,
features.

Email: **sales@houseofstratus.com** please quote author, title and credit card
details.

OTHER TITLES BY HENRY CECIL AVAILABLE DIRECT
FROM HOUSE OF STRATUS

Quantity		£	$(US)	$(CAN)	€
	MUCH IN EVIDENCE	6.99	11.50	15.99	11.50
	NATURAL CAUSES	6.99	11.50	15.99	11.50
	NO BAIL FOR THE JUDGE	6.99	11.50	15.99	11.50
	NO FEAR OR FAVOUR	6.99	11.50	15.99	11.50
	THE PAINSWICK LINE	6.99	11.50	15.99	11.50
	PORTRAIT OF A JUDGE	6.99	11.50	15.99	11.50
	SETTLED OUT OF COURT	6.99	11.50	15.99	11.50
	SOBER AS A JUDGE	6.99	11.50	15.99	11.50
	TELL YOU WHAT I'LL DO	6.99	11.50	15.99	11.50
	TRUTH WITH HER BOOTS ON	6.99	11.50	15.99	11.50
	THE WANTED MAN	6.99	11.50	15.99	11.50
	WAYS AND MEANS	6.99	11.50	15.99	11.50
	A WOMAN NAMED ANNE	6.99	11.50	15.99	11.50

ALL HOUSE OF STRATUS BOOKS ARE AVAILABLE FROM GOOD BOOKSHOPS OR
DIRECT FROM THE PUBLISHER:

Hotline: UK ONLY: **0800 169 1780**, please quote author, title and credit card details.
INTERNATIONAL: **+44 (0) 20 7494 6400**, please quote author, title, and credit card details.

Send to: **House of Stratus**
24c Old Burlington Street
London
W1X 1RL
UK

Please allow following carriage costs per ORDER
(For goods up to free carriage limits shown)

	£(Sterling)	$(US)	$(CAN)	€(Euros)
UK	1.95	3.20	4.29	3.00
Europe	2.95	4.99	6.49	5.00
North America	2.95	4.99	6.49	5.00
Rest of World	2.95	5.99	7.75	6.00
Free carriage for goods value over:	50	75	100	75

PLEASE SEND CHEQUE, POSTAL ORDER (STERLING ONLY), EUROCHEQUE, OR
INTERNATIONAL MONEY ORDER (PLEASE CIRCLE METHOD OF PAYMENT YOU WISH TO USE)
MAKE PAYABLE TO: STRATUS HOLDINGS plc

Order total including postage:_____Please tick currency you wish to use and
add total amount of order:

☐ £ (Sterling) ☐ $ (US) ☐ $ (CAN) ☐ € (EUROS)

VISA, MASTERCARD, SWITCH, AMEX, SOLO, JCB:

☐☐☐☐☐☐☐☐☐☐☐☐☐☐☐☐☐☐☐☐☐☐☐☐

Issue number (Switch only):

☐☐☐

Start Date: Expiry Date:

☐☐ / ☐☐   ☐☐ / ☐☐

Signature: _____

NAME: _____

ADDRESS: _____

_____

POSTCODE: _____

Please allow 28 days for delivery.

Prices subject to change without notice.
Please tick box if you do not wish to receive any additional information. ☐

House of Stratus publishes many other titles in this genre; please
check our website (**www.houseofstratus.com**) for more details